Little Angel Helper

a novella

Bria Burton

Soul Attitude Press

Published by Soul Attitude Press
PO Box 1656
Pinellas Park, FL 33782
www.soulattitudepress.com
soulattitudepress@gmail.com
Cover Artist: Bria Burton
Angel glyph from Pixabay.com, edited by Bria Burton
www.briaburton.com

ISBN 978-1-939181-71-8

First Edition

ACKNOWLEDGMENTS

I'm blessed with an incredible writing community, especially through the Florida Writers Association. Some fellow writers I'd particularly like to thank: John Rehg for your expertise and help in creating the print version of this book; Cate, Alice, Rachel, Sue, and Seth for your incredible critiquing abilities and your encouragement; Maria and Martin for your willingness to read my stuff and spur me on.

My family is a lifelong blessing. A never ending stream of gratitude flows toward each of them: my husband, who patiently perseveres with me while loving me and supporting my writing habit; Mom and Dad who are my forever fans and the ones who always taught me to strive for my dreams; Aunie, who inspired this story and makes me laugh and constantly teaches me about life; Larisa, Philip, and the girls who give me so much love and encouragement; Mom and Dad Burton who treat me like a daughter and whom I treasure. A general thanks to all my Gomez and McFarland relatives for your constant love, affection, and support. I'd like to particularly thank Aunt Elena and Aunt Kelly for your kind words after you read this story.

Thank you, Jesus, my Lord and Savior, for the way you mold me and shape me every day. I wrote this story because I believe that every life is precious, and that God takes extra care of the people in this world with special needs like my sister, Aunie.

For my sisters, Larisa and Aunie

1.

Bradley Hunter didn't need a security guard to escort him out of the building. He wasn't going to cause a scene. The calm, even gentle way he loaded a few items from his cubicle into a box should've assured the guard that his presence wasn't needed.

The boss had insisted it was policy. Nothing personal. Just like the firing hadn't been personal. It was a tough economy and layoffs happened. Unfortunately for Bradley, his name was under a solid, red line like the rest of the accountants missing the all-important CPA license. This firm was downsizing, and being very nearly licensed (final test in two weeks), wasn't good enough.

With the guard flanking him, Bradley made his way to the elevator, arms wrapped around the box, light as if he carried a couple of kittens. The items inside, not kittens, hopped around with all that room. His buddy, Drake, patted his shoulder on the way out. "Raw deal, man."

"Thanks." He forced a smile knowing it probably looked like a misshaped melon slice.

"Drinks on me tonight. Eight thirty." Drake raised his coffee cup, taking a sip as if already starting.

Bradley gripped the box in one hand while pressing the elevator button. He glanced over his shoulder. "Can't tonight," he said. Not unless he got lucky today. It wasn't likely, not with things starting out like this. Desperation didn't usually work in his favor at the casino.

"Friday, then." Drake saluted, turning and striding back toward his cubicle.

Bradley didn't want to be jealous, but he couldn't help it. Drake was a full package kind of guy. Tall, athletic, often mistaken for Kobe Bryant, and married to a Swedish model with an adorable set of twins. Earned and kept his place at the firm while Bradley was jobless, had no one even resembling a girlfriend, and was headed to an empty apartment where rent was overdue. Then there was the whole gambling addiction thing, which he could admit was a problem. At the moment, he had bigger problems, so he wouldn't address that one until later.

The security guard rode with him to the lobby. Even when Bradley said he could find his way out, the guard followed him all the way to the door. As he reached for the handle, ready to push, a familiar voice called his name.

"Bad-lee!"

The high-pitched, tone-deaf squeal stopped him dead in his tracks. He turned and saw Marie jump to her feet from the lobby chair she had been sitting in.

His sister was here? But she wasn't supposed to be coming until tomorrow. After this morning, he had planned to call Paulina, whom he presumed was the woman seated in the chair next to where Marie had been, and let her know this wouldn't work out after all. The timing couldn't be worse.

Marie loped over to him, hugging his back, arms squeezing his stomach too hard. She had trouble gauging appropriate levels of . . . anything.

"Sissy!" He set down the box to give her a proper hug. She reached her arms high, wiggling her fingers like jazz hands. Her hair was shorter than he liked, a bowl cut with blunt bangs that made her look twelve. Whoever cut her hair should try harder to make her look at least slightly more age-appropriate.

He wrapped her up the way she liked, his hands locked behind her, picking her up and dropping her fast. She squealed with delight, patting his neck hard.

"New Yok!" She hopped up and down, her pronunciations a little better than when he last saw her.

"Tall sky-pers. I love you, Bad-lee." She kissed his cheek, a smooch that left a wet spot behind.

"I love you, Marie." He picked up his box, panic setting in. This wasn't going to work out, and he hated to do it, but he had no choice. He had to send her back to Kansas.

2.

Paulina Robart had seen pictures of Bradley at the Hunter household, but never met him in person. His formerly lanky frame, which barely held up the shoulder pads of the football uniform he wore in one of the pictures on Mrs. Hunter's mantel, had filled out. Not too much. Beneath the gray suit, he still seemed fit, like he worked out regularly at a gym. His face, slightly broader, was much the same, and full of delight the moment he laid eyes on his sister, Marie.

When he bent to pick her up in a bear hug, lifting her off her feet and gently setting the giggling girl down again, Paulina felt a calm washing over her. Everything was going to be fine. Marie would be so happy living with her much bigger, slightly younger, brother. He was thirty-five, if Paulina remembered correctly. Marie was two years older.

The way Mr. and Mrs. Hunter had talked about Bradley,

he was a gem. Top of his high school class, graduated magna cum laude at Columbia, always well-liked but didn't get into much trouble. Certainly never caused Mrs. Hunter grief the way some boys did to their moms. When Marie talked about her "big bo Bad-lee," she came alive with excitement. It was Marie's way to shout with joy, clap her hands, and dance when anything pleased her. It was one of the most refreshing things Paulina ever experienced, someone getting so excited about their brother, and equally overjoyed when receiving an ice cream cone. No need to hold back, let the joy flow forth! Life was meant to be enjoyed. Marie taught her that.

Technically, Paulina was the teacher, but people like Marie made her feel like the student. After students graduated from a special-ed high school, they weren't technically students anymore. Paulina wasn't technically a teacher. At the Topeka Action Center for Adults (TACA), students were referred to as members, and teachers as guides. The program as a whole functioned like a school. There were no residents, members arrived to their designated homerooms at eight in the morning, and left at three thirty in the afternoon Monday through Friday. Most of them were bussed to and from home. But the program goals focused less on learning new material like a typical school (very difficult for some members) and more on engaging the senses, interacting with others, basic life skills, and contributing to society. Marie and some of the more advanced members spent one day a week working at a local McDonald's where they earned a small income.

For as long as Paulina could remember, she'd wanted to work with people with special needs. The calling, while rewarding, had its share of heartaches, but she wouldn't trade her job for any other position in any of the skyscrapers in New York.

This trip was Paulina's first time serving as an escort, traveling on a plane from Topeka to NYC with a TACA member. When she had learned of Marie's circumstances, she didn't hesitate to volunteer. From Marie's first day, she felt a special connection with the blue-eyed, bouncing beauty. If Marie didn't speak, most people would never know about her developmental delay. She was a perfectly healthy woman, no physical handicaps. Wonderfully cared for and provided for at home (sadly not the case with all members).

The sudden deaths of Mr. and Mrs. Hunter shocked and saddened everyone at TACA. Tragic car accident. Marie had been confused and agitated, difficult to handle that day. A kind neighbor took her in for the foreseeable future, but no one had been able to reach Marie's closest remaining relative, her brother, Bradley. He hadn't kept in touch much with anyone, hadn't visited in years. But one high school buddy had tracked him down at the office where he worked to give him the terrible news.

Bradley had agreed to let Marie come and live with him in his apartment in New York City. He had a spare bedroom. His willingness to take responsibility impressed Paulina, and seeing him interact with Marie erased most of her worries. The hardest part would be saying goodbye to that darling girl.

Paulina rose from her seat in the lobby of his office building with an extended hand. "I'm Paulina. So nice to meet you."

Bradley reached around Marie, who held onto his arm, shaking Paulina's hand. "You, too. But I thought you were coming tomorrow."

The brightness in his face, that look of joy from seeing Marie, faded. No longer smiling, he bent to pick up a box, which gave Paulina pause. A security guard had been walking with him a moment ago, as if escorting him to the door. Did he just lose his job? Paulina was afraid to ask.

"I guess there was some mix up," said Paulina, trying for light-hearted. "We had a taxi bring us here when you didn't meet us." The red-eye flight had been smooth, both she and Marie had slept, but his absence at the airport worried Paulina. Now the box in his hand, the look on his face, and the words coming out of his mouth elevated that worry to anxiety.

"I can't do this."

3.

Bradley couldn't stand the look of disappointment Paulina aimed at him. He was simply telling the truth, he couldn't do this. Not now.

"What do you mean, Bradley?"

Did he really have to say it in front of Marie? His sister might not understand a lot of things, but she felt rejection like anybody else did. Bradley didn't want her to feel rejected by her own brother, but he didn't know if there was any way around that.

Paulina's expression, worn like a tragedy mask, stabbed at his heart, made him feel the full extent of how terrible it was to even suggest an inability to care for Marie. Paulina was one of the employees at TACA, Marie's program, but Bradley had never met her and knew almost nothing about her. He guessed she was Latina from the bronze hue of her skin to the thick, almost black hair in a loose ponytail to the deep, brown eyes. As a person who helped those with special needs as a career, she couldn't fathom Bradley's decision to back out on his sister. It would be beyond her comprehension almost as much as it was beyond Marie's.

"Can we discuss this on the cab ride to the airport?" With Marie holding his hand, and while hugging the box with the other, he pushed through the door. He waited for Paulina to come through, but she stood dumbfounded.

"The airport?"

"I just . . ." Bradley didn't know how to word it better than *I can't do this.*

"Sir, please don't prop the door." The security guard came toward them.

"Our luggage." Paulina pointed where she and Marie had been sitting. Three rolling suitcases, one very large, rested upright beside the chairs.

"I can assist you with your luggage to the curb," said the guard.

Inside, Bradley handed Marie off to Paulina, not making eye contact with either of them. Marie made little noises and spoke random words, some he couldn't make out. She repeated "New Yok," several times and something that sounded like "little anger hipper."

He couldn't engage with her right now. They used to play this game, back when he lived at home, where he'd pretend to repeat what she was saying, and he'd purposely choose a different but similar sounding word. If she said, "I want cake now," he'd say, "You want fake cow?" She'd laugh and slap his arm. "No! No! No! Not cow!"

He placed his box on top of the large suitcase. With the handle up, he tipped the luggage back onto its rollers and the box stayed in place. The security guard picked up the two smaller suitcases by the short handles, lifting and carrying rather than rolling. Paulina held the door open. Marie stayed by her side, bouncy on her toes and giggling.

Bradley followed the guard across the sidewalk, navigating through a few pedestrians. Horns honked. Behind him, Marie imitated the noise. The delicious smells of the pizza place next door wafted down the block, making him hungry. At the curb, the security guard set down the luggage, nodding to them and walking back to the building where Bradley was no longer employed.

"Excuse me, Bradley, but we aren't returning to the airport. My flight home isn't until tomorrow evening, you may recall." Paulina stood in front of him with Marie at her side, her tone firm. "Marie and I can share the bed in your spare room tonight as we originally discussed. I'd appreciate it very much."

With a wave, he hailed a cab, not sure how to respond. He didn't like the idea of Marie unpacking her suitcase or

Paulina helping her put clothes in the closet. She'd come expecting to live with him. With Paulina's help, he may be able to convince Marie this trip was a visit, not a move. Would Paulina be willing to help? For his sister's sake, he hoped so. "All right."

"Bradley, did you lose your job?" She spoke softly, genuine concern in her voice and eyes. It was the kind of tone that she probably used with Marie or any of the other TACA students.

Marie gazed up at the skyscrapers, oohing and aahing. She hadn't heard Paulina, who spoke low.

"Yes. Now you know why I can't keep my word. This trip has to be just a visit. I'm—" He didn't want to apologize. If they convinced Marie this was a vacation, he'd have nothing to apologize for.

A yellow taxi pulled up beside them. The driver popped his trunk. Bradley loaded the suitcases while Paulina helped Marie into the back seat. "I'm sure you'll have no trouble finding a new job. You're an accountant, right? There must be plenty of opportunities to choose from in New York." Paulina slipped into the cab.

Bradley slammed the trunk closed. She wanted to change his mind. This was not going to be a fun cab ride.

4.

On the way to Bradley's apartment, Paulina encouraged Marie to take the window seat while she sat in the middle between the two siblings. At first, Marie tried to engage Bradley, reaching over Paulina to tap his leg. She chittered like the birds that perched outside Paulina's bedroom window every morning. Paulina understood Marie a little better than the birds, but when she got excited, she babbled mostly unintelligible words. Bradley responded with smiles and assenting noises, but Paulina thought he must not know what she was saying. While the sights and sounds of Manhattan kept Marie's attention directed out the window, Paulina took the opportunity to discuss with Bradley the serious dilemma he had presented.

"Bradley," she whispered, leaning toward him. He smelled nice. His cologne was woodsy with a hint of bottled sunshine. Marie still wasn't paying attention to them, so Paulina probably didn't have to whisper. As they pulled up to a stoplight, a guy dressed as a teddy bear outside a toy store kept Marie preoccupied. "This must be a really difficult day for you, and I'm very sorry about your job. But your sister needs you."

Bradley stared out the window. His knee bounced like he was agitated, yet he looked calm. He must be thinking.

"I'm so sorry about your mom and dad. But don't you think they'd want you and Marie to be together?"

He stopped shaking his leg. He faced her frowning. "Not if I can't take care of her the way she needs. Look, I get that you've got my sister's best interests at heart. And I appreciate all that you've done. But living with me is not what's best for her. I lost my job. I'm not stable financially. There has to be someone else who can take her."

Paulina sighed. "There isn't. If you don't sign the paperwork I brought, she'll become a ward of the state. And that's not best for her. Trust me."

When Paulina visited the group home where some TACA members lived, she always got the sense that the couple running the place cashed their government check and spent the money on anything but the people in their charge. It was always dirty inside, and smelled only slightly better than a sewer. The members didn't often get bathed or fed properly except at TACA. If the group home owners decided that someone was beyond their capacity, they'd have them committed to a mental institution. But some of the people they sent away were by no means difficult to care for, and should've been able to stay in the group home. Paulina visited the mental hospital once, and she found it difficult to go back again.

If she could've kept Marie herself, she would have. After nineteen years as a TACA guide, she'd had numerous people she'd wanted to take home with her. But unlike Bradley's situation, hers made it truly impossible. She cared for her alcoholic mother, making her place unsafe for anyone else to stay.

She would do everything in her power to keep Marie out of that group home. She'd fight for Marie, and convince Bradley to sign those papers. "I spent days going back and forth to the guardianship agency, making sure I had everything in order so that you could be your sister's guardian, not the state. It's not going to be easy. But I can tell you love your sister very much."

"I do," he said. "It's out of my hands now. I was already worried about being able to provide for her before I lost my job. Now it's impossible."

"Trust me, it's not. You'll get another job. And you'll have a lot of help." Paulina squeezed his arm, hoping to reassure him. She didn't have the paperwork in front of her where she'd made copious notes, but she knew most of it by heart. "She's covered under Medicaid, and I found five doctors near your apartment who accept that insurance. You'll never have to worry about health coverage for her. On tax forms, you'll be able to claim her as a dependent. In walking distance from your place, I found an adult program accepting new members. It's very similar to TACA. They can pick her up and drop her off, and they are open seven days a week. Not all members attend on weekends, but it's available for those who need it. They also provide references for sitters. When you've got plans, you'll never have to leave Marie by herself."

"It's just not possible," he snapped. "I'm sorry." He covered his face, and then rubbed both hands through his hair. It was light brown like Marie's.

"Bad-lee?" Marie reached over Paulina to touch his knee. "O-K Bad-lee? Lil angel huppa here. Don't wor-wee."

"Yeah, I'm okay, Marie." He patted and held her hand. "What did she say? Little angel what?"

Paulina was surprised that he needed her to interpret. "Little angel helper."

"What's that?"

"Lil angel huppa, Bad-lee. Dare!" Marie pointed at the space between Bradley and the passenger seat ahead of him.

He glanced around the cab. The driver jerked to a stop at a light. They all lurched forward before settling back into the seat. "What is she talking about?"

Something about Bradley's ignorance didn't sit right with Paulina. As long as Marie had been coming to TACA, she'd talked about her little angel helper. On her first day eighteen years ago, she had mentioned him, and on most days since. "You've never heard her say that before?"

"No," he admitted, releasing Marie's hand. Another costumed figure on the street corner had stolen her attention away.

"Well," Paulina began, trying to find the best way to describe it to him, "it's actually pretty amazing. Marie says that she has a little angel helper that God sent to her. She acts like he's a person she can see."

"Like a guardian angel?"

"Yes. In fact, this angel has performed a few miracles."

"What?" he asked, raising a skeptical eyebrow.

Paulina knew how crazy it sounded, but she'd been a witness to some unexplainable things. "I'm serious. If someone at TACA loses something, Marie can usually help them track it down. Last month, a member lost his rabbit's foot key chain. Marie's little angel helper led her to it."

"Maybe she's got a sixth sense or something." Bradley

folded his arms, shaking his head. "I don't believe in angels."

"That time your mom had the seizure, Marie was the only one at home. Nobody could figure out who had called 9-1-1. Later, when your dad investigated, the police department couldn't find a recording of the call. The operator remembered it, though, and said a man's voice told her a woman was having a seizure and said the address. Marie had been telling your mom and dad that little angel helper had used the phone." Paulina raised her palms.

"Somebody must've come to the house and made the call," Bradley insisted.

"They checked with neighbors, the UPS guy, even created a Facebook page to try and find the man who'd helped them. Nobody has ever come forward." Paulina squinted. "Didn't they tell you about that?"

"No."

That seemed strange. Mrs. Hunter had never had a seizure before, and never had one since as far as Paulina knew. Why wouldn't they have told their son about it? "I have to admit, I do believe in angels. Not just because of Marie, but she's the reason I've lost any doubts."

Bradley shifted uncomfortably. "When should we tell her that this is a visit, not permanent?"

The cab stopped abruptly, all three of them lurching forward again. They had arrived at Bradley's apartment.

Paulina had no intention of telling Marie any such thing. She had less than forty-eight hours to convince Bradley to sign those papers, and she wasn't giving up. "Let's just look over the paperwork inside, and we'll take it from there."

5.

Paulina was kind enough to offer her credit card to the cabbie, a beer-bellied, scruffy-faced guy with gray sprouting throughout his dark, wavy hair like weeds on a lawn. "I'd like to pay for Marie's expenses as long as I'm here," she said. Even though Bradley knew she was doing it to change his mind, he really appreciated it.

The gray building with white trim stood seven stories high. Bradley's apartment was five stories above where they exited the cab. Although not luxury condos, the place was nice enough. Somewhat generic, but he wasn't big on décor or expensive furniture. As far as living space, having his needs met satisfied him. He had the essentials, and everything he'd found on Craigslist pretty much matched. The spare room was almost never used. Drake slept over once after a celebratory night of drinking in honor of the birth of his twins.

When Bradley had first agreed to become Marie's guardian, he bought a new pink bedspread for the spare room with colorful flowers all over it. He'd been excited to show it to her then, but now he dreaded the thought of her getting attached to something she couldn't keep. Maybe he could ship it to wherever she ended up living.

Out of the cab, Marie oohed and aahed as if the place was as magnificent as the Empire State Building. "Wow! Nice house, Bad-lee!"

"Thanks, Marie." She didn't really grasp the concept of apartments versus houses. Neither Paulina nor Bradley corrected her.

The driver popped the trunk. Bradley lifted his box out first, setting it on the curb, then the heavier suitcase. Once everything was upstairs, he'd head to the casino.

The way his luck ran, he knew he shouldn't go, but he didn't know what else to do. He needed to pay his rent today or his landlord would tack on a late fee. After two months of late fees, he'd be evicted.

Marie hopped around the sidewalk clapping, singing, "Tinkle, star! What are?" But with the r's not quite pronounced.

"I'll get you two inside, and then I have somewhere I need to be."

Paulina lifted the last suitcase out of the trunk. "We'll

come with you."

Two steps away from the cab, the suitcases rolling behind him, Bradley stopped. "Not a good idea." He faced her. "I'll be back in a few hours."

She slammed the trunk closed. "We're coming." Her dark eyebrows raised in a "do not argue" manner that reminded him of his ex-girlfriend. Paulina was a strong personality like his ex had been. Hence why they hadn't worked out. He didn't like being bossed around.

Paulina leaned her head into the passenger window, probably asking the driver to wait for them.

Bradley used to leave his cell phone and a couple bucks in the seat to convince cabs to wait, that he'd be good for the fare. But he was out of cash and no longer had a cell phone. His gambling debt, now a whopping $4,850, had made it impossible to keep up with the bill. His only phone was his office line. Now he didn't even have that.

"I'm taking the subway. A lot cheaper." The only reason for the cab in the first place was the inconvenience of the suitcases. A taxi only shaved off twenty minutes of travel time to the casino. Not enough to make the fare worth it.

"We still have things we need to discuss." Paulina pulled out her credit card again, the sunlight glinting off the VISA insignia. "I'll pay for the ride."

He hated being in such a vulnerable financial position.

But if she wanted to waste her money on cab fare, and waste her words on deaf ears, fine. The extra twenty minutes might be worth it in this case, especially since he wouldn't have to hurry back home to them. "Okay. Have it your way."

After dropping off the suitcases and a very brief tour of his place, Bradley trying to downplay the pink comforter despite Marie's delightful squeals, they were back in the cab.

Bradley sat in the middle between Paulina and Marie. When he announced, "Resorts World Casino," as their destination, he glanced at Paulina.

Her eyelids briefly expanded, the subtlest hint of her surprise. Otherwise, she was silent. Maybe she regretted her insistence now knowing they were headed to a casino. She had a folder in her hand. No doubt, guardianship papers were inside. Bradley expected her to immediately delve into the folder, give whispered speeches, but she remained quiet. He hoped her resolve was crumbling.

Everything outside awed Marie. She chatted to people on the sidewalks who couldn't hear her. She wiggled, her proximity to Bradley frequently causing her movements to bump his left leg and hip, but he didn't mind. His building shrank in the rear view mirror. Without a job, Bradley couldn't afford his place, let alone another mouth to feed.

True, he'd probably have no trouble finding a new job. Paulina was right about that. He'd been scanning the online employment boards and classified ads in the paper for places hiring CPAs to keep his options open, having no idea it would become a necessity. Plenty of firms were hiring. Not the one he'd had his eye on since moving to NYC, the Packer Group, but there were several reputable firms where he'd be content. He'd be a CPA in two weeks barring catastrophe—failing the last test would be catastrophic. He did well on the other three. No reason to think he wouldn't pass.

Even with that in mind, it was just crummy timing. The next two weeks would likely involve more borrowing. Even if he got a job right away, it would take many paychecks to get himself out of the mess he'd gotten into. There'd be nothing to spare for quite some time. Rice and beans were on the menu indefinitely. Maybe in six months or a year he'd be back on track, in a good place where he could ask for custody of Marie. But he wouldn't even mention that idea until then.

If things went well at the casino, which he dared not hope, there was a slight chance that he could consider having Marie stay. But his luck would have to exceed probability. Otherwise, he had no choice but to stick with his decision. Marie would become a ward of the state.

He didn't like it, but he had no other choice. He only wished he could do more than gamble for a miracle. The way Paulina made it sound, nobody would be picking out nice comforters for Marie. Wasn't there anybody else? He knew there wasn't. Dad's one brother was dead, and Mom's one sister was in a nursing home somewhere. They'd both had kids, cousins Bradley barely remembered meeting as a child, and Paulina had already spoken to all of them. None were willing to take on Marie. They weren't in her life either. Just like Bradley hadn't been for so long.

He couldn't believe his mom had a seizure and they never told him. Had they tried? Probably. Bradley couldn't blame them. For years, he hadn't returned their calls. He hadn't gone back to visit since leaving for college. Not once. He really hated Kansas. They visited him twice while he was at Columbia, but he hadn't made them feel welcome. Because he knew that they knew.

They'd known. They had to. He'd felt too guilty to keep up the relationship. Rather than admit what he'd done and apologize, he pretended that he didn't get along with them and wanted nothing more to do with them.

The money he took from their account was for something so stupid. His freshman roommate had this idea for a social media site where members would post ten second video clips of anything, and people could comment.

He wanted kids to be able to use it, so no pornography would be allowed. Decreasing societal attention spans would draw people to TenSeconds.com.

It never got off the ground because neither of them knew how to build a social media site. The computer programming major they found who said he could do it asked to be paid a one-time $10,000 fee, which would include any site updates for as long as they kept it running. The roommate assured Bradley that they'd earn back triple that amount in the first week. Since his parents would get the money back right away, Bradley had given the answers to the security questions on their account. The guy took the money without doing a thing and apparently fled the country.

Now Bradley's parents were gone. He lost his chance to apologize. The only thing he could've done, care for Marie, was out of his hands.

His sister started in on "lil angel huppa" again, repeating the phrase over and over, pointing at Bradley's lap.

"Is there anything I can say to convince you?" Paulina wasn't whispering like Bradley had expected. She actually sounded defeated.

His destination had given him away. He lost his job *and* he was a gambler. He wouldn't be good as a guardian for Marie. Paulina was starting to understand.

"Probably not."

Paulina pursed her lips. "Do you think . . . ?" She hesitated. "I believe . . ." She stopped, didn't finish her sentences.

"I hope to win big," said Bradley. But he had no expectations.

6.

A casino? Of all the places Bradley "needed" to be, that was the last place Paulina would've ever imagined. He gambled? How regularly? Is that why he wasn't doing well financially?

In the back seat of the cab that smelled like feet, she laid the folder with the guardianship papers in her lap, unsure how to convince him to sign.

The light and cheery way he'd said, "I hope to win big," had stunned her into silence. She tried not to criticize people, but when confrontation was needed, she rarely hesitated. That's why she and Marie were in this cab. It was all she could do not to pounce on him for such a foolish decision on the day he was fired. Did he really think the casino would solve his problems?

In this case, Paulina didn't know Bradley well enough to say anything. Honestly, she didn't know much about his circumstances. For all she knew, this was a one-time thing because . . . he was feeling lucky?

No, she feared he had real money problems. That his quickness to abandon Marie was based on that, not because he didn't want to help.

In the middle seat, he chatted with Marie, teasing and tickling. Her high-pitched laugh bubbled out. She was as happy as Paulina had ever seen her. Especially since Mr. and Mrs. Hunter had died.

Paulina couldn't allow her resolve to weaken. All things considered, Bradley was still a better option for Marie than the group home. It was never going to be ideal with their parents gone.

The red numbers increasing on the cab's meter felt like a punch to the gut. Paulina couldn't watch. She turned to look out the window, the streets crowded with buildings and people. Not like Kansas. They crossed the Bronx-Whitestone Bridge, a toll road. The amount due flashed on the meter as the cab passed through the express lane, adding to her total. No more peeking. She'd wait until she got home to assess the damage on her credit card bill.

So sure that all Bradley needed was time with Marie, not away from her, Paulina had offered to pay for the ride to wherever. She liked being generous when she could, and she needed to keep the conversation with Bradley going until he agreed to keep Marie. She couldn't do that if he was off somewhere while she and Marie were alone in his apartment.

Now she felt foolish. He'd planned to take the subway. They could've all done that. The taxi had seemed like the best way to have another conversation where it was just the three of them, no other distractions.

Paulina lost all her ammunition as soon as he named the destination. She needed a new approach. What would it take? She had to get him to admit what specifically held him back and see what could be done.

They rode on and on. How far was the Resorts World Casino? She didn't want to know. All the traffic jams made it feel like an eternity.

When they finally pulled into the covered entrance of the cream building that probably lit up colorfully at night, she handed her card over to the driver without looking at the total. Bradley and Marie exited through their side, cheering and whooping together.

Paulina retrieved her card from a hand with dirt under the fingernails, thanking the driver and stuffing the receipt and the folder into her purse. She got out and followed the siblings inside through the glass doors. Marie wrapped her arm around Bradley's. She pointed out everything. The size of the lobby, the escalators, the gigantic, glittering chandelier that reminded Paulina of an extravagant silver gown the way it draped from the high ceiling.

It was only eleven in the morning, but plenty of people wandered around. Men in suits like Bradley, women in nice dresses, some tourists that wore outfits similar to what Marie and Paulina were wearing—jeans, comfortable shoes, long sleeves, and jackets. Some parents even had their children.

Maybe Paulina was overreacting. She knew plenty of people who blew off steam with a trip to the local casino. That might be Bradley's only intention. Seeing him engage with Marie gave her hope. He was great with her, and obviously loved her.

Bradley led them into the food court. Marie immediately honed in on the ice cream shop. "Peez, ice keem?"

"Later," Bradley said, patting her arm as he released her. "It's a little early. Maybe get some food first like a cheeseburger over there." He pointed at the *Queens Burgers* sign. "Or a sub at Subway. Or pizza. Mmmm." Bradley rubbed his belly. "That's what I want when I come back."

"Yeah, pizza!" cried Marie, waving at the people serving at the Artichoke Bastille's Pizza counter. One of the guys waved back, smiling. Marie covered her giggles with her hand.

"Sure," said Paulina. "We can all eat pizza together. When you get back. My treat." She looked him square in the face, watching his expression turn serious. He'd been cheerful with Marie, but Paulina was his reality check.

"Thanks," he said, straightening his tie. "That'd be great. I won't take too long. An hour." He glanced over his shoulder where the entrance into the casino glittered, bells and whistles beckoning for everyone twenty-one and up to come in and join the fun. "Maybe two. At most."

"Bradley." How to word it? She didn't want to be pushy, as much as she came here to do just that. Push him until he gave in. "What will it take for you to sign the papers? Seriously. I want to know. I want to help."

Beside her, Marie was still flirting with the guy at the pizza counter, who was playing along, shyly waving and smiling, making her laugh.

Bradley bowed his head, shaking it. "That's not why I'm here. I'm hoping to make enough to pay the rent that's due today. As for the papers, I'm sorry. You won't change my mind."

"Something will." Paulina believed that had to be true. "You wouldn't want to see your sister in that group home, trust me. So what would it take? Is it a dollar amount?"

Bradley lifted his gaze and scratched his forehead, squinting. In that moment, he resembled Marie—the way she looked when someone asked her to pick between Skittles or M&Ms. "I guess if I managed to pay my rent and some other . . . outstanding fees that I owe, I might reconsider. But it's a lot. More than I could win in a couple hours."

"How much?"

"Over six grand."

Less than Paulina guessed. But probably more than he would win now, that was true. "What if I started a fundraiser? I could organize a bake sale back home, or a walk—"

"No, no." Bradley waved his hands in front of Paulina. "I'm not a charity case."

"But Marie is," Paulina insisted.

"And I need the money today, the rent at least, or the amount will keep climbing, and I could lose the apartment. Seriously, Paulina, I know the position I've put you in, and I'm sorry." When he swallowed, his Adam's apple bobbed. "I think while I'm in there, you should start breaking the news to her. Explain that this vacation will be over tomorrow evening, and she'll be going back with you."

She didn't want to tell her that. Everything inside of Paulina screamed out against it.

He stepped over to Marie, squeezing her shoulders. "I'll be back soon for pizza, okay?"

"Kay!"

As he strolled away, toward the casino, Paulina clasped her trembling hands together. This might be one of those hopeless situations. No matter what she did or said, Bradley wasn't going to sign the papers. She hated feeling helpless. Her life's purpose was helping people like Marie who couldn't help themselves. It broke her heart, but Bradley was right. Marie needed to be told the truth.

7.

Need more time?

The message popped up on the ATM machine. Bradley was still debating the dollar amount to withdraw. Even with all the arcade sounds surrounding him—*dings, bada bings, wowzas,* and other obnoxious bell progressions—he thought he heard Marie's laugh coming from the food court where he'd left her with Paulina.

No, that was all the way across the casino. Too much noise for that to be possible. He was hearing things in his guilt-ridden head.

Paulina was getting to him. When he thought she'd given up on asking him to sign the guardianship papers, finally accepting that his answer was no, he'd been mistaken. Not that he cared about disappointing her, a practical stranger, but she was more concerned about his own sister than he was. What was wrong with him?

He didn't like feeling guilty. Usually he ignored those emotions. That's how he ended up with two deceased parents who had no idea how sorry he was for shunning them, not to mention the stealing.

Bradley pressed *YES*. The screen reverted, ready for him to enter a withdrawal amount again. He'd done a balance inquiry first. $1,100 left. That was it. All the money he had. In order for the account to remain open, he needed a $100 minimum balance, so only $1,000 could be withdrawn.

The $1,500 he owed in rent today would become $1,800 tomorrow when his landlord tacked on the $300 late fee. Best he could hope for at the casino was $500 in winnings. With rent paid, he could worry about the rest—his gambling debt, his need for a job—later.

Take out $500 and hope to double it, or gamble the full $1,000 and have a higher probability of winning the extra $500?

Need more time?

He jammed his finger into the screen, annoyed that it kept asking him that.

YES.

The accountant side of him knew this was the stupidest, worst habit he could've ever formed. That side now had company. The side that wanted to do right by Marie.

He needed a reason beyond himself to stop coming here.

The responsibility of caring for his sister could give him that. If he lost now, there was always the future. He could give Marie, and Paulina, that hope. In six months, maybe a year, he'd get out of debt and be ready to sign the papers. Marie could then leave the group home and come live with him permanently. She could last that long, right?

He pressed *1-0-0-0*, and what he entered read as *$1,000.00*. He hit *OK*. One last roll of the dice (pun intended). Was there a chance for him to make enough money to sign those papers? Of course, there was always a chance, however small. Whatever happened, this would be his swan song as a gambler. And then he'd be done. For good.

8.

At one of the food court tables, Paulina checked her cell phone, surprised she hadn't heard from Mamá. Humming, Marie colored with the crayons Paulina had brought. The sheet of paper came from one of the restaurant counters. Marie had scribbled all over the menu in red, blue, purple, brown, and green. Now she was adding yellow.

The screen of Paulina's phone showed three missed calls from *HOME*.

Shoot. The cell had been on silent. After a brief pause of consideration, she left it on silent and put it back in her purse. Mamá could wait. She was probably calling because she lost the TV remote and couldn't be bothered to walk across the room where the buttons on the TV itself worked just fine.

She mentally slapped herself. *Not nice. Don't be so harsh on her.* Her mother had it rough her whole life, and had done her best, even in the midst of her addiction, to provide for Paulina. Alcoholism ran in the family. The least Paulina could do was be respectful. However, time away was always nice. Even this trip with all its difficulties granted a pleasant reprieve from her mother's demands.

The casino noise drew Paulina's gaze. She couldn't see Bradley beyond the slot machines. His request had incensed her. How could he ask her to break the terrible news to his sister? He wouldn't take any other responsibility when it came to her, so the least he could do was tell her himself.

Another mental slap. *Stop being so cruel. He's in a tough spot. Give him a break. He's trying in his own way.* And he obviously had a problem. Maybe even an addiction. She knew more about that than she liked.

"Pay game?" Marie asked for the fifth time, pointing with the yellow crayon now tipped with an array of other colors.

A claw vending machine sat in one corner. A surprisingly long line of children waited to play what Paulina considered an unwinnable game. She didn't like the idea of Marie playing if she couldn't win, and had told her no, that nobody ever got the toys. "You don't really want to play, do you?"

"Yes!" Marie had contradicted. "Pay, peez? Lil angel huppa n me."

Some of the kids, after failing to retrieve anything with the claw, went to the back of the line to try again. It seemed strange that parents would allow their children to spend so much money on this rigged machine. But then again, the parents were probably inside gambling themselves.

"Pitty peez?" Marie's sideways grin with a few crooked teeth showing softened Paulina. Really, what would it hurt? In life, people lost all the time. This trip was the perfect example. They had nothing else to do while waiting for Bradley.

"The line is long. If Bradley comes back, we might have to leave before you get a chance to play. Okay? And just one turn."

"One! Yes!" Marie stood, clapping.

Paulina gathered the crayons into the plastic bag and put them in her purse. As they walked, Marie carried the colored menu. They entered the line. Twelve kids ranging in age from about six to fourteen were ahead of them. In no time, more joined the line behind them. It was the only game in the food court. Maybe that explained the great number of children willing to repeatedly play the awful game.

A pair of boys cheered on the teenager who currently attempted to win something. They were chanting, "Egg! Egg! Egg!"

Paulina craned her neck to see.

The majority of the prizes were stuffed toys. The teen was trying to grab a giant, plastic purple Easter egg. The claw apparently captured the egg where it sat on top of a stuffed gorilla, but as soon as the claw lifted, the egg slipped out of its grip.

No surprise there.

The teenager tore at his hair, spinning in a circle while the others made "awww" sounds, some patting his back. "This is rigged! You all know that right? It's impossible to win the egg." The teen faced the line, speaking as if he owed it to them to share the truth.

"I'm gonna win it!" cried the girl ahead of them.

"No, me!" another boy shouted.

"Candy egg?" asked Marie, shaking Paulina's hand with excitement. "I wanna egg!"

"You can try, Marie. But don't get your hopes up, okay? Everyone else wants it, too, and nobody has gotten it so far." Why weren't any of them aiming for the stuffed toys? At least they had a better chance with those.

"Lil angel huppa, candy egg!" Marie addressed the invisible figure above them.

Paulina grinned. That would be the only way anyone could win that slippery thing. A miracle. Maybe Marie should send little angel helper into the casino to help

Bradley.

She shook her head. As much as she believed in Marie's guardian angel, she didn't think that's how he worked.

One child after the other tried, but all failed to capture the egg. The girl in pigtails ahead of them suddenly cried, "Dang it!" It wasn't even her turn.

Paulina raised her eyebrows.

She was no more than eight, and staring at an old flip phone. The clothes she wore smudged in places. Her hair seemed unwashed. "I gotta go. Mom's waitin'. You want my token? I ain't gonna win." She held out a dirty hand toward Marie. A gold coin rested in her palm.

Paulina hadn't noticed that the machine only took tokens. "Thank you. That's very sweet, but I'll pay you for it. Is it fifty cents?"

"Dollar."

"Okay." Paulina handed her four quarters. "What do you say, Marie?"

"Oh! Tank you!" Marie took the gold coin, her high-pitched squeal making the girl step back.

"What's wrong with her?" she asked.

"Nothing is wrong. This is Marie. She's very excited and thankful. That's how she shows it. Do you know what it means when someone has special needs?" asked Paulina, well-versed in this type of conversation.

"Like, she's retarded?"

"In Marie's case, we say developmental delay."

"Because retarded's a bad word?"

"No. It's not. But some people say it to be mean. So we like to use other ways to describe the special needs Marie has."

"Oh, okay." The girl smiled, jogging away. "Bye, Marie! I hope you win."

"Byebye!" She waved, the colored menu flapping, but her focus was on the gold token in her other hand.

From the direction the girl ran, Bradley strode toward them. Was he already done with the casino? He looked . . . upset was putting it mildly. His face was red, his tie undone.

Paulina realized this might be a good moment to return Mamá's phone call, give Marie and him a few minutes alone. They could play the game together.

She stepped forward to meet him. "Bradley, I need the restroom. Will you help Marie when it's her turn?"

"Um . . ." He seemed off-balanced, distracted. "Sure."

"I haven't told her yet. I think you should." Before he could react, she turned to Marie. "I'll be right back, okay, Marie? Bradley is here to help you."

"Bad-lee! Hi!"

He put on his happy face for his sister. Paulina headed

for the restroom, dreading the conversation with Mamá only slightly less than the conversation she and Bradley would likely be having soon.

9.

"Bad-lee, candy egg!" In one hand, Marie held up a gold token with the casino's logo engraved on it, and a menu that she had apparently been coloring in the other.

"Candy egg?" He wasn't sure if the coloring was supposed to be an egg or the token. It was difficult for him to concentrate on anything. And it was really hot. He'd loosened his tie. Now he undid the top button of his shirt. "Neat, Marie. I like it."

"No!" She pointed to the claw vending machine. A kid was attempting to pick up what looked like an Easter egg.

"Oh, you want to win that egg." *Good luck trying to win anything here.* But he didn't say that. He repressed his bitterness and disappointment for her sake.

Had Paulina really not told Marie that she wasn't going to be living with him? He couldn't be upset with Paulina. This was all on him. He was a crappy gambler and brother.

He could finally admit it. After losing the full thousand in less than an hour, he walked away resisting that voice begging him to borrow more, the one assuring him that he would win big next time.

No more. He'd promised himself it was the end, and he was going to make Marie a new promise. The group home would be temporary. Eventually, he'd bring her back to live with him. He had a rough six months or so ahead, but he'd straighten himself out and make a home for Marie that Mom and Dad could've been proud of.

Marie was next in line to play. "Here, I'll hold your coloring." He took it from her, folding the paper and tucking it into his jacket pocket.

"Lil angel huppa n me." She clapped, hopping up and down.

"Don't worry. A retard won't win."

Bradley stiffened, turning around at the sound of a teenager's cracking voice. Behind him, two punk boys folded their arms across their chests. "What did you just say, kid?"

The one on the left with a girlish haircut grunted while his friend nudged him. "I meant that I'm not worried about her getting the egg before I get a chance to try."

Bradley restrained the hand that had closed into a fist, pressing it to his side. He really wanted to swing and knock the smug expression right off this punk's face. Kids these days respected no one, and they were cruel. Still not a great idea to hit him. Thankfully, Marie didn't seem to hear. She was still hopping and clapping, awed by the boy playing the game. "Really? We'll see about that. And you owe my sister an apology."

"Whatever. She doesn't even know what she's doing." He gestured toward Marie. She was at the machine, moving the claw aimlessly.

"Whoa, hold up, Marie. Let me help." Bradley stepped forward, wondering how she figured out how to start the game all by herself. She moved the joystick wildly, laughing. The claw jerked back and forth above a pile of stuffed animals and her desired prize: the candy egg.

"Okay, Marie, if you want the egg, you've got to—" Bradley felt a tap on his shoulder. If that kid was purposely trying to distract Bradley, so help him.

A casino employee stood beside Bradley with her arm stretched out like she wanted him to follow her. "Please step aside, sir. No assistance on the Casino Claw." Her accent and dark skin implied she was from somewhere in the Caribbean.

"Huh?" Was she serious? "My sister needs help. She's—"

"I heard what that little brat said." She gestured toward

the punk kid, glaring at him. Bradley glanced over, and he was glaring back at her.

"You can't call me that!"

"Oh, but you can call names? Nuh-uh. I don't think so, Stan. I know your mother. You *will* apologize to that young lady when she's done."

He scowled. "Fine."

"I can't help her?" asked Bradley. "At least show her how to drop the claw?"

"Looks like she's got that figured out." The employee nodded toward Marie.

When Bradley looked, he was surprised to see the claw descending over the Easter egg. "Hey!" He stepped forward. "Good job, Marie."

"Yeah! Lil angel huppa. Candy egg!"

"Stay right here, sir. No helping."

Annoyed, he took a step back. "I can cheer her on, right?"

"Yes, you can. From here. But no coaching."

This was so weird, but Marie was doing fine without him so he didn't argue further.

The claw closed around the egg. The boy before her had gotten that far, and the egg had slipped right out of the claw's grip.

As Marie moved the joystick, the egg wobbled in its

grasp. Bradley cringed. "You can do it, Marie. Keep trying."

The claw slowly lifted. The egg remained cupped in the claw's hand. It lifted the egg all the way to the top.

Several astonished gasps erupted from the line of children, all watching Marie in awe. Bradley kept quiet now, not wanting to startle her.

Please, God, let her win. It's all she wants right now. And maybe it will soften the blow when I break the news to her.

Bradley didn't usually pray, but it seemed like the right thing to do at the moment.

The claw slowly made its way across the sea of stuffed animals. The egg was tipping. It moved like it might fall out.

Just hold on!

The egg slipped and fell.

Cries of lament echoed throughout the food court. Bradley's heart sank.

As the egg fell from the claw's grasp, it hit the edge of the wall that kept the stuffed animals in—the wall that opened into the winning chute. The claw had been moving toward that opening, giving the egg enough momentum to bounce off the wall and drop into the victory slot.

"Yes!" Bradley threw up his hands at the same moment

that Marie did. He charged her, picking her up and spinning her in circles. He felt her giggling, heard her screams of joy. The lights in the room changed, flashing and dancing like when someone won a jackpot in the main casino. Everyone was on their feet, cheering.

Bradley set Marie down. "Candy egg! Lil angel huppa did it!"

"He did, huh?" Bradley still wasn't sure about angels, but Marie had won after he prayed. Maybe there was something to that.

"Congratulations, young lady." The employee walked over carrying the egg, and ushering Stan forward with a firm grip on his arm. "Well?" She raised a thin, black eyebrow.

He bowed his head. "Sorry I called you that name."

"Tank you!" Marie reached out, hugging him.

The boy lifted his chin, his eyes wide like no one had ever hugged him before. He patted Marie's back, then stepped away and walked off.

"Here is your prize. Marie, was it?" The woman handed the egg over, smiling wide. Bradley appreciated her warmth and tenderness.

"Yes!" Marie cradled the big egg like a baby.

"All this over some candy?" Bradley scratched his head, gazing at the crowd clapping and smiling at them. The lights still danced and flashed.

"Sir, this egg doesn't have candy in it."

10.

After assuring Mamá that she would be home in two days, as promised, Paulina hung up the phone and used the restroom. She wondered if Bradley had told Marie the truth yet. Would she be crying hysterically? Paulina prepared herself for the inevitability that the rest of this trip would be a challenge. Not only in keeping Marie as calm as possible, but staving off her own disappointments when it came to Marie's future. Little by little, the group home would stifle Marie's spirit as it had so many others. Soon she would become a shell of her former, lively self. It was too depressing to think about now. At least Marie would still come to TACA and receive plenty of love and affection there. Paulina just hoped the group home owners wouldn't find an excuse to commit Marie to the mental hospital. That might send Paulina's spirit beyond the breaking point.

Back in the food court, the quiet scene had changed.

Colorful lights spun across the room like a disco. People were standing, cheering. How strange? She thought that only happened inside the casino. Everyone faced the claw machine in the corner. One of the children must've won something. Actually, this was neat. What a great way to make the kids feel special.

As she crossed the room, maneuvering through the crowd and searching for Marie in the long line of children clapping, Paulina spotted her in the most unexpected place.

In front of the claw game, Bradley lifted Marie high, spinning her in circles. Paulina gasped. Had Marie won something? All this celebration was in her honor?

Delighted, Paulina rushed over, clapping. "Marie! Did you win?" By the time she arrived at Marie's side, the precious girl held the giant Easter egg she had wanted so badly. "Hooray, you did it! You won the candy egg. I'm so proud of you." She wrapped her arm around Marie's shoulder, squeezing and pressing her cheek to Marie's.

"Lil angel huppa did it." She grinned her sweet, sideways grin, both eyes wide and reflecting all the colorful lights.

Paulina knew that must be true. *Thank you, little angel helper, for being so sweet to Marie.*

"Will you say that again, please?" Bradley raised his voice at a casino employee. The woman with stylish, tight black curls resembled Viola Davis, the actress from the movie, *The Help*.

Paulina noticed he was smiling, not upset. "Bradley?" She reached for his shoulder, tapping it. "What is it?"

Still facing the employee, he lifted a hand, his pointer raised. "One sec, Paulina."

"Sir, one moment." The employee's tag read, *Regina*. She turned aside, speaking into an earpiece with a Jamaican accent. "Marie is the name."

A voice came over the loudspeaker, a Casey Kasem type. "Well, ladies and gentleman, this is quite an historic moment. A young lady named Marie has just won our quarterly promotional prize at the Casino Claw in the food court. She is the first person to ever win the coveted prize. Congratulations, Marie!"

More cheering, clapping, and whistles from the crowd. The colored lights faded until disappearing, and the normal lighting returned.

"What I said before," Regina continued, "is that the egg contains our quarterly promotional prize. A legal guardian must accept the winnings on behalf of a child under eighteen, or a person with special needs. But only one person at a time can attempt to win the prize. That's why you couldn't help or coach her. Haven't you seen our ad on TV?"

"No," said Bradley. "So what's the promotional prize?"

"Six thousand, five hundred dollars."

Goosebumps raised on Paulina's arms and legs, even beneath her jacket and jeans. Her mouth opened involuntarily, and her brain took longer than usual to process what had been said.

$6,500.

Unless she misheard. "Excuse me, what?"

"What?!" Bradley cried, slapping his forehead.

"The placeholder cash is inside that egg." Regina gestured toward Marie's prize. "Casino-made bills. You pick up the real cash on your way out. Our recommendation is that you have us wire the money to your bank account. If you prefer cash, we offer an employee escort to your vehicle, to one of the shuttle buses which services the nearest subway station, or to a taxi. We also offer a limo service for a fee."

"Do you mind if I open your egg, Marie?" Bradley held out his hands. She placed the egg in his palms.

"Candy now!" She laughed and clapped, bouncing on her toes.

He split the egg apart. Inside, six rolls of what looked like Monopoly money rested in the lower half, one slightly thicker than the others. He picked up the rolls, one at a time, handing them to Paulina. "Will you keep these in your purse?"

"Awww. No candy?" Marie frowned, folding her arms.

Paulina stared at Bradley, slowly nodding. She accepted each roll, placing them in the inside zipper pocket of her handbag. She and Bradley silently exchanged wide-eyed, questioning glances. What did this mean? Would Bradley change his mind now? This was exactly what he said he'd needed.

"If you'd all get together," Regina waved them back toward the claw machine, "we'll get a picture."

A photographer stood nearby, camera at the ready.

On either side of Marie, Bradley put an arm around her shoulder, and Paulina rested a palm on her lower back. Bradley gave the egg back to Marie. She raised it up.

"Not blocking your face, hon," said the photographer. "Down a little. Or higher. Okay, that works. Now let's see that big smile . . . cheese!"

"Cheeeeeez!" Marie echoed, holding the egg overhead. Paulina held her grin during the flash, but might've blinked.

"Congrats!" he said.

"Tank you!" said Marie. "But no candy?"

The photographer chuckled. "I bet you can buy lots of candy now!"

"Can?" She looked to Paulina, who nodded.

"Of course. We'll get you some candy soon."

"Kay."

"Where do we go when we're ready to leave?" asked Bradley.

Regina pointed toward the open doorway that led into the lobby. "Out that way, the first window on your left. Tell the woman at the window you're there to pick up the quarterly promotional prize, and she'll lead you to an office where someone will help you. Congratulations, Marie."

"Candy soon," she replied, smiling.

"Well, Marie, how about that pizza and ice cream? I bet we could get them to put some candy in the bowl. How about that?" he asked.

"Yeah! Candy n ice keem!"

Back at the same food court table where Paulina and Marie first sat down, Paulina and Bradley enjoyed their pizza. The huge, four-cheese slice with pepperoni melted in Paulina's mouth. She'd never had genuine New York-style pizza before, and it was the best ever. Hands down.

Marie dove into her ice cream bowl that was sprinkled with M&M's and pieces of Heath bar, leaving her pizza on its plate. Paulina and Bradley let her.

"Thanks again for this." He raised his slice in a *cheers* gesture.

"Like I promised, my treat." *Now what about you and*

your promise? Paulina hoped Bradley would bring it up first, that she wouldn't have to keep nagging him. With this new turn of events, wouldn't he finally come around?

"What do we do now?" He arched his eyebrows.

She wasn't sure exactly what he meant. "With the prize? Whether it's best to leave with cash or wire the money?"

"I guess. I don't even know if we can do either unless . . ." Bradley finished chewing, swallowed. "This is Marie's money. I'd never take it away from her. But a legal guardian has to pick it up. Won't it be impossible for us to get the money unless I sign the guardianship papers?"

Oh, Bradley didn't know. The guardianship agency had given Paulina temporary custody of Marie for this trip. It was valid until Bradley signed his part, taking over the custody. Or until Marie became a ward of the state.

The temptation was there, and Paulina couldn't help but roll it around in her mind. She could leave out that piece of information, and Bradley would sign for the sake of getting Marie her money. It was in Marie's best interest for Bradley to use the money to pay off his debts so she could live with him. Did Paulina really have to convince Bradley about that part?

As for the other, Paulina abhorred dishonesty. Withholding information was as awful as a boldface lie. The only reason she didn't think it worth mentioning before was because it had no effect on the situation at hand like it did now.

Better to tell the truth in the first place before it came back to bite later. "I'm her legal guardian until you sign or until she becomes a ward of the state. I can sign for the money."

Bradley raised an eyebrow. "Oh. Okay." He ate, but said no more.

Paulina finished her pizza before breaking the unbearable silence. "The amount you said that you needed, that would make you reconsider signing the papers—"

"I know." He took his last bite, swallowed, and wiped his hands on a napkin. "This whole time, I swear I've been reconsidering it. But it just doesn't seem right. I was talking about the money I won, not someone else."

"What do you think Marie would want to do with that money?" Paulina paused, holding back her answer, as desperately as she wanted to say it for him.

"We should give her some options, I guess. Let her know she can buy some nice things at her new place. Be really comfortable there."

"She'd be infinitely more comfortable with you. And she will tell you that herself if you ask her." Paulina had no doubt.

"I'd be a rotten brother if I took her winnings."

"No, I don't think of it that way. To pay the rent at her new place, where she wants to be? To erase the debt that would prevent her from being able to live with you? Instead, to be placed in a miserable, dirty, and unloving group home?" Paulina couldn't believe he was torturing himself like this. "Ask her."

The corners of Marie's mouth held smudges of chocolate as she took her first bite of pizza.

"Marie?" He faced her timidly, as if afraid of her answers, whatever they might be. "You won some money when you got that egg. Do you know what you would like to do with it? What do you want to buy?"

"Pink bed." She spoke while chewing, the pizza rolling around in her mouth. "I like."

Paulina resisted the urge to add her own leading questions.

"The bedspread I got for you? You like that?" he asked.

"Yep. Seep pink bed."

"Seep?" He glanced at Paulina for interpretation.

"I think she's saying she's excited about living with you and sleeping with the pink comforter you bought," said Paulina, hoping to be helpful and not obnoxious.

Bradley sighed. "Yeah. Um, Marie, what about spending the money you won? You already have the pink bedspread. Do you have anything else you'd like to buy?"

"No." She chewed, swallowed, chewed again.

Paulina tilted her head. "Trust me, Bradley. All she wants is you, her brother. To live with you."

"Marie, would you be upset if I spent your money for you? To pay rent and take care of some things?"

"You buy it. Lil angel huppa sez you."

"What?" Bradley looked to Paulina again.

"I think she's saying little angel helper wants you in charge of the money." She clasped her hands on the table. "Listen, Bradley, this is very honorable of you to get Marie's input. But you realize that a legal guardian is in charge of her money."

"I know that. But—"

"Typically, you won't ask her opinion of things to buy. You'll help her pick out stuff, sure, but you're basically the parent and she's the child."

"I don't know if I'm ready to do that." He dropped his gaze, elbows on the table, hands clasped behind his neck.

"Fair enough. But you're the one who said what it would take. 'Over six grand.' Your words. Low and behold, here it is."

"I know." He raised his hands, smiling. "It's crazy, right?"

"I think it's providential."

He didn't disagree. Neither of them spoke for a few

moments.

"You n me n little angel huppa." Marie touched his gray jacket with her hand, leaving behind some ice cream and pizza grease.

"Here." Paulina dug into her purse, pulling out some wet wipes. She circled the table, ready to rub it off.

"Thanks, I got it." He took the wipes, dabbing his jacket sleeve, grinning wide.

She wasn't sure if the grin was a good sign or a bad sign. "Will it come out?"

"Of course it will. I'd better get used to this, right?" He lifted his gaze, meeting Paulina's.

His smile reached his eyes, and she understood. "You'll sign then? Become her guardian?"

"Yes. You win, Paulina. You win."

11.

In a casino food court, of all places, Bradley officially became his sister's keeper. Paulina beamed, even watered up. After the possible intervention of an angel—he really couldn't knock it now—Bradley had felt moved to act. The money Marie won would allow him to keep his promise and take care of her. Paulina was right, he shouldn't think of it like he was taking her winnings away. The rotten brother move would've been making Marie go back to Kansas. Thanks to her little angel helper, he could turn things around and make a home for her that would in no way resemble the miserable alternative.

Yes, he'd been absent from her life lately. Yes, he'd been a terrible son to their parents. She didn't seem to hold anything against him, and he had a chance to make up for it. Not only by caring for her, but by being a good steward of his—no, *their* finances from now on. She was his only family, and they should stick together. Not to mention how much he loved spending time with her. He couldn't have handled sending her away now, even if he'd felt guilt-ridden about the money. He would miss her too much.

Inside the office where they had been directed to collect Marie's winnings, a pretty woman in a red dress and an up-do hairstyle congratulated his sister. "I'm so happy that you won! That game is so difficult, I'm absolutely amazed. You are quite a talented young lady."

Marie's crooked smile widened, her giggles erupting erratically. She shifted back and forth, rubbing her arms.

Bradley gave a nod of appreciation for the kind words.

Paulina retrieved the casino money from her purse and gave the woman each roll.

After scanning copies of the freshly signed guardianship papers, she handed Bradley a few forms. "For the IRS."

"No problem. I'm an accountant."

"Now for the fun part." The woman clasped her hands together, winking at Marie.

She tried to wink back, but closed both of her eyes.

"The total prize amount is sixty-five hundred dollars."

Although it was hard to believe, Bradley didn't need to pinch himself. It was real.

"You have several options. Cash in a lump sum, which we do not recommend for obvious reasons."

"New York muggers?" Paulina offered.

"Sadly, a reality. And also the possibility of losing the money between here and your bank. We cannot offer any kind of compensation due to the loss of a cash payout. We recommend wiring to an account. Simple, should be accessible within twenty-four hours, and—"

"Wait, you mean the money won't be accessible immediately?" That wasn't good. Bradley needed it today.

"They put a hold on these types of winnings, yes. But at," she pointed to the clock on her wall, "one o'clock tomorrow, your account should reflect the increase. If not, you can call us to check and make sure there are no problems with your bank."

"Actually, I'd like to take the cash in a lump sum, please." Paulina eyed Bradley, obviously surprised and dismayed by the decision. He had an idea. "How much is that limo service?"

In a town car, cheaper than an actual limo, Bradley, Paulina, and Marie sang, "The Wheels on the Bus." Both Bradley and Marie were equally off-key. Paulina had a nice singing voice, and helped them get back on track. Bradley enjoyed adding incorrect lyrics, like saying the wheels go zig and zag.

"No! Not ziggy." In the middle seat, Marie laughed, slapping his leg hard and fast.

He didn't stop her. The sting was worth it to see her riled up. "They don't go zig and zag?"

"No! Wound and wound!" Her mouth widened as if demonstrating the roundness of the wheels.

"Ah, yes. Got it, got it."

Back at his apartment, he asked Paulina if she could keep Marie entertained for about two hours. "I'm dropping this off for my landlord. Fifteen hundred." He laid the amount, paper clipped, on his coffee table. "And this will erase everything else I owe. Four thousand, eight hundred, and fifty dollars." He slipped that amount into an envelope. He didn't add that it was all gambling debt. Paulina could probably figure that out. He'd be free and clear, and would not be returning to the casino.

From Marie's suitcase, Paulina lifted out a board game. "Marie, how about Candy Land?"

"Yeah! Candy-and!" She raised her arms high, skipping around his living room.

Marie was already bringing some much needed joy into his life. He was so happy that she'd be living with him permanently.

Bradley redid his tie while staring at the wall mirror. "I'll start making appointments for job interviews tomorrow. In a couple weeks, when I hopefully pass the final CPA exam, I should have no trouble getting hired somewhere if I haven't been already."

In the reflection, Paulina knelt on the carpet, setting up the game on the coffee table beside the cash, but still looked up like she was listening. Marie sat on the floor across from her, ready to play.

"And if I'm already employed, they'll give me a raise or I'll find someplace that will." Something pleasant came to mind. "Hey, and I'll be getting my last paycheck from my previous job next Friday."

"That's great, Bradley. I'm really pleased to see how everything is working out. I know you'll find a job soon. Tonight, if you want, we can go over the information I briefly mentioned. The adult program, the health insurance. Oh, and Marie's typical routine. Bedtime, how she likes her eggs, all that."

He faced Paulina, glad she had turned out to be so stubborn and persuasive. "You've taken care of Marie for a long time. Thank you. Especially for this last little bit. I'll never forget it."

"You're welcome." She grinned, her brown eyes gleaming. She turned to Marie. "Which piece do you want?"

"Geen."

Bradley picked up the cash. He stowed both stacks in his inside jacket pocket like he'd done when leaving the casino, and said goodbye for now. The town car, still waiting to take him to his next destination, cost ninety-five dollars. Worth it to keep the cash safe. All that remained, fifty-five dollars, he slipped into his wallet.

The landlord was home, dressed in a white tank and sweat pants that had been hemmed mid-calf, probably by his wife. He lived on the first floor. Bradley handed over the money. The landlord seemed pleased. "Not usually cash from you," he said in his Greek accent.

"Making sure I don't owe that late fee."

"Right, right." He waved the paper clipped stack as he closed his door.

As Bradley exited the building, the cool breeze, along with his relief, washed over him. Rent paid on time. Check. No need to worry about that anymore.

The town car dropped him off at Pauly's Laundry Service in Brooklyn. "Thank you." He tipped the driver five dollars, grateful that the fee covered two stops. Although no one in New York had ever attempted to rob him, he couldn't take chances right now.

Inside, he stopped at the front counter. Couldn't hurt to keep using their laundry service, right? They'd done miracles last time with an old spaghetti stain on one of his white shirts. "Can I drop this off?" He unbuttoned his suit jacket, pointing at the sleeve where Marie had wiped ice cream and pizza grease. "Just a little stain."

The scraggly, dark-haired young man, the same one who'd been there every time Bradley had come in, retrieved a coat hanger from one of the nearby racks. "No problem."

"Also, I have something for Mario." He took the envelope out of the pocket before handing over the coat.

After draping the jacket on the hanger, the young man gave Bradley a laundry slip, gesturing with a head nod. "He's there. Go on back."

Bradley side-stepped the counter, walking through a sea of hanging clothes in plastic bags. The door in the back was ajar. He knocked.

"Come!" A gruff admittance.

Pushing in, Bradley approached Mario, who spun around in an office chair. His desk faced the wall paneling. The beady eyes always made Bradley uneasy. Mario wore his typical brown leather jacket and jeans with cowboy boots. The gray at his temple salted his black as night hair, gelled back as if with a slick comb. "Got something for me?"

"This is all of it." Bradley gave him the envelope, and then took a few steps back.

Mario squinted at Bradley before dropping his gaze. He flicked open the unsealed flap, fingering the cash, apparently counting.

Bradley didn't know why, but he suddenly felt nervous. Anxious, at least, to get out and never come back. Except for his jacket, of course. One of his former coworkers had recommended this place as an acceptable means of borrowing without using a bank, and Bradley would never thank him for it.

A large, muscular tank at least seven feet tall entered and walked past Bradley. "You hear about Lenny and the garbage truck? Man, that boy can run." Thick, Brooklyn accent. Arms like an Olympic body builder.

Now Bradley was really nervous.

Mario, his accent less noticeable, waved the tank over. "You remember Bradley, don't you, Pauly?"

Pauly? As in the owner?

"No, I don't think I've had the pleasure." Beside the desk, he folded his arms in front of him, not smiling.

"Hi," Bradley said, unsure whether to offer a hand to shake. He took his body language as a cue and simply nodded. "Nice to meet you. Is this your place?"

"Technically, it's my father's. He's a bit old to run things now, so I do most everything."

"Ha!" said Mario, still counting. "Sure, you do. In that case, you mind double-checking Bradley's numbers for me? I'm concerned this might be short. Last name?"

"Hunter," said Bradley, not liking the sound of Mario's

assumption.

"Give me a sec." Pauly turned and walked toward the back of the office, exiting through a door that led to who-knows-where.

The tie felt like it was choking Bradley again. "I'm an accountant, so I'm pretty sure it's all there." At Mario's glare, Bradley stuttered, "B-but of course, double check. I don't expect you to know what I owe you off the top of your head."

"What's the amount?" Pauly stuck his head back inside, but didn't open the door any further.

"Four-eight-five-zero."

"That doesn't account for thirty percent interest."

"*Thirty?*" Bradley's palms were clammy. He wiped them on his suit pants. "No, it was ten percent. And I did account for that."

"Ten?" Mario guffawed. "Pauly, do we ever offer anybody ten percent?"

"I wouldn't offer that to my mother." He leaned back, stepping out of view. The slit in the doorway revealed another office-like room.

Heat enveloped Bradley. Sweat dripped down his back. A throbbing ache began behind his eyeballs, moving into the back of his head. Could they be messing with him?

"What's the difference, Pauly?" asked Mario, dropping

the envelope onto his desk. Some of the bills slid out. "What's he still owe?" He stared at Bradley, his expression dead serious.

"Checkin'," the disembodied voice replied. "Eight eighty-three."

Bradley's heart sank to the floor. They weren't messing around. This was how the game worked. They played him for the fool he was for coming to them in the first place. "My friend, Charlie, recommended me to you. When we met, you said—"

"Stop." Mario hoisted himself up using the armrests of the chair. "You want to tell me about what *I* said?" He stepped closer. Bradley didn't move. Not one inch. "I'm disappointed. You still owe us eight hundred and eighty-three dollars, Bradley. You come in here claiming things but not delivering. I should up your interest just for that." Mario's index finger neared Bradley's face. His breath smelled like peppermint Altoids. "Instead, you know what I'm gonna do? Since you seem to have no trouble collecting dimes, I'm giving you a deadline." He dropped his hand, moving it into his jacket pocket.

Bradley could only imagine what was inside. Knife? Gun?

"Twenty-four hours. You deliver what you owe, and I'll forget your disrespect. If not, I'm adding thirty percent every day until it's paid." Mario backed up slowly, returning to a seat in his chair. "I don't have to tell you what might happen if you let that debt keep climbing, do I?"

"No." It wasn't a veiled threat. Mario's pocket was shaped like a pistol and told Bradley all he needed to know. Mario would never admit that ten percent was the initially agreed upon interest. There was no negotiating with him. Bradley was trapped under Mario's thumb, and he wouldn't let him out easily. "Here." He reached into his pants pocket, hands shaking as he retrieved the cash from his wallet. He held out two twenties and a ten. "All I have on me."

Mario snatched the bills, tossing them onto the envelope like they meant nothing.

"I'll get the rest. By tomorrow." He would have to. Who knew what they'd do to him if he didn't?

"I hope that's true, Bradley, for your sake." Mario spun around, facing the desk. "Now scram."

It was an out-of-body experience walking back through the Laundromat. A spinning rack swung a dress at him. Bradley jumped out of the way, dodging any other hostile clothes items, and sped out the door.

His body turned automatically. He walked on the sidewalk toward the nearest subway station. He knew the route by heart. The pain in his head felt like someone slammed a crowbar against the back of his skull. Images flashed by, his mind playing out scenes of a grim future.

Mario raising the pistol. Pauly slipping on a pair of brass knuckles. The guy up front wielding a bat.

What about Marie? Did they know about her? A sick, hollow pit formed below his sternum. His entire body trembled. He couldn't handle the thought of them using her as leverage or bait or whatever else they might be capable of doing. They couldn't find out he had a sister or she'd be in danger, too.

"NO!" Bradley kicked a garbage can, knocking it over. A few women scurried out of his way. He tore at his hair, ripping some out. How could he have let this happen? He'd been so incredibly stupid.

Sitting on the subway train, staring off and seeing nothing in front of his eyes, Bradley knew the terrible truth. His foolish choices meant Marie was already in harm's way. It was too dangerous for her to stay. He had to go back on his word *again*. She'd have to go back to Kansas.

12.

A scraping, clicking sound came from Bradley's apartment door. Someone put a key in the lock and was turning it.

"Bradley's back!" said Paulina, eager to discuss all the things he'd need to know regarding Marie and being her guardian.

"Bad-lee?" Marie clamored to her feet, a hand on the coffee table for leverage. "He-uh?"

"Yes, I think he's here." After three games of Candy Land, Paulina was ready for a break, and some adult conversation.

Marie scurried to the door. On her tip toes, she swayed back and forth, waiting for him to come in.

As the door opened, Bradley's wild hair drew Paulina's attention first. Then his lack of a suit jacket over the button-up shirt and tie. But the look on his face concerned her the most.

His down turned mouth. His eyes, encircled with redness. The way he looked at Marie with sadness. Or was it regret?

"What's wrong?" Paulina was on her feet, bracing herself for something terrible. She didn't know if she could handle terrible news. Not when her worst fear, Bradley changing his mind *again*, seemed like the only thing that would make him appear the way he did right now.

Bradley slowly pushed the door closed, locking it behind him, never taking his eyes off Marie.

"Bad-lee!" She hugged her brother, and he squeezed her tight, closing his eyes.

Paulina waited. There was nothing else to do.

When he finally let go, Marie patted his cheek with her hand. "O-K?"

Even Marie could tell something wasn't right.

"Marie, I have something to tell you." He kept his focus on her alone. He wasn't even glancing at Paulina. "I'm very sorry, but you're not going to be able to stay here. Paulina will take you back to Kansas. But I'll send the bedspread to your new home, okay?"

"Stay? You n me n lil angel huppa." She was pointing to the empty space next to Bradley. "Dare. Lil angel huppa."

"Little angel helper will take good care of you in your

new home. Okay?"

"Home." She pointed at the floor.

Paulina couldn't stand to be left out any longer. "Bradley, please. Tell me what happened."

He directed Marie to the couch. "Do you want something to drink, Marie? I think . . . no, wait. I only have water."

"I got us some water already." Paulina gestured to the glasses on the coffee table coasters.

Bradley lifted the glass that was Marie's and handed it to her. "Here."

She took the water, sipping. "Home?" She pointed at the couch.

He caught his reflection in the mirror. Without answering, he smoothed down the hair that was sticking up.

"Did you have trouble with your landlord?" Paulina tried, knowing that probably wasn't it. The $4,850 had to be gambling debt. If he used a loan shark, Paulina hated to think of all the possible reasons that Bradley would back out on Marie now.

"It's bad, Paulina. I made some really foolish choices, and I have to pay for them." Finally, he turned his defeated gaze toward her. "I can't allow Marie to suffer for my stupidity."

"Please tell me. I might be able to help." On the couch,

Paulina sat beside Marie, who still sipped slowly, slurping.

Bradley slumped into the cushioned chair beside them. "I got involved with the wrong kind of people. They are saying my debt isn't paid, even though I gave them everything I owed, plus the last fifty dollars from Marie's winnings. Now they want another eight hundred and thirty-three dollars by tomorrow." He paused, sighing. "I have one hundred in the bank. That's it. There's no way I can pay it in time. They'll increase my debt every day I don't pay. Eventually, they're going to . . . " He glanced at Marie " . . . do harmful things. I can't have her here when that day comes."

"My God, Bradley." Paulina pressed her fist against her beating heart. It was as bad, no, worse than she feared. "You have to call the police."

"I don't think that will help." He leaned back in the recliner. "What do I tell them? Some guys say I owe them money, and implied what they would do to me if I didn't pay? They didn't come out and say anything specific. I'm afraid the police won't be able to do anything. If they question these men, they'll probably come after me and do even worse because I was a snitch or whatever."

This was beyond Paulina's realm of understanding. In all her life, she'd never experienced anything like gangster movie material. There had been rough patches with her mother, but nothing comparable to men threatening to hurt, maybe even kill her over debt. She had no idea what to suggest, or what could help Bradley.

His decision to protect Marie would mean they were right back where they started this morning. He'd sign her over to become a ward of the state, and she'd be stuck with the group home. An amazing miracle had happened, and Bradley had come around because of it. Was everything hopeless now?

"I'm so sorry, Paulina. I wanted Marie here. I still do. But not like this. I can't risk her safety."

Paulina understood that part. "What if I loaned you the money? I have a four hundred dollar ATM withdrawal limit, but I can take out that much today and again tomorrow morning. You can take out thirty-three dollars from your own account—"

"Actually, that would cause my account to be closed if I fell below the hundred dollar minimum." He shook his head, resting his hand on her knee. "But that's not why I'm saying no. It's because I don't want you involved with this either. I hate what I've put you and Marie through today, and I won't make it worse. This is my problem, and I have to solve it. But thank you." He leaned back again.

A tingle in Paulina's chest moved down into her stomach. She felt like his hand had imprinted on her leg.

For a moment, she couldn't look up at him, feeling a little vulnerable. Which was silly.

She lifted her chin, embarrassed that she'd wondered if he meant something by the touch. Of course he didn't. He was at the bottom of a barrel, not thinking about anything but the terrible mess he was in. She felt so sorry for Bradley, and desperately wanted to help. She only had a little more than a thousand in her own bank account, but wouldn't let him know that. Maybe he was right, her involvement wasn't a good idea. But how did he plan to pay off these men? Or what was he planning to do if he couldn't? It wasn't her place to ask, but she really wanted to know.

Marie set her empty glass on the table with a loud clank.

"Gentle, Marie," said Paulina, moving the glass onto the coaster.

"Lil angel huppa. Dare!" She rose from the couch, pointing. "Dare!" She ran around the coffee table and into Bradley's bedroom.

"Marie?" Bradley and Paulina stood at the same time. She followed him into his room, wondering what Marie thought she saw.

Marie faced Bradley's closet. "Ate. Fee. Fee."

"What, Marie?" Bradley asked, stepping beside her.

Paulina studied her face. In front of the closed closet

door, Marie stared slightly upward like she usually did when "talking" to little angel helper.

"Ate. Fee. Fee," she repeated.

Was she counting something? "Eight, three, three?" Paulina tried.

"Yeah." She smiled. "Dare." With her middle finger, she pointed at the closet. "Lil angel huppa. Dare."

"Eight, three, three." Bradley squinted. "Marie, you want me to open the closet?"

"Eight hundred and thirty-three. Like what you owe," Paulina said. How had Marie remembered that? She didn't usually pick up on details of long conversations very well.

"Ate. Fee. Fee. Dare." She continued pointing.

"Am I getting this right? Little angel helper is telling Marie there's money in my closet?"

"I . . ." Paulina started to speak, but hesitated. "I don't know. Usually he helps people find what they lost. But you didn't lose that money. Well, I guess you did lose it at the casino. And look what happened there with the egg. You got what you needed."

"Except it wasn't enough after all." Bradley opened the closet door. The walk-in wasn't very big, but neatly organized. He stepped inside. "Okay, Marie. Now what?"

"Dis." She squeezed past him, making Bradley back up into his hanging clothes.

Paulina couldn't see what Marie was doing at the shelving in back.

Bradley lifted a pair of jeans and showed them to Paulina. "He apparently wants me to wear these."

Marie pushed past Bradley and came out to stand by Paulina. "Yes!" She clapped.

"Put them on?" Bradley asked.

"Maybe try the pockets?" It was a stretch, but Paulina had no idea what else little angel helper would have in mind.

He searched each one, pausing with his hand inside the right front pocket. "Whoa."

The brightness in his eyes made Paulina gasp. "What?"

He drew out a green bill. "Twenty bucks." He shrugged. "Must've forgotten it. Thanks, Marie. Tell little angel helper thanks for trying."

"Trying?" Did Bradley really not trust his own eyes? "How could Marie have known those jeans had money in them?" Another miracle. Paulina wouldn't call it anything else.

"No, I know. It's amazing. A gift, at least. Maybe an angel really is here. But it's not eight, three, three."

"Maybe there's other money that you don't remember." Paulina couldn't help but let her hopes rise higher and higher. After all she'd witnessed, she believed little angel helper was about to offer another miraculous solution to Bradley's problems. "Think about it. No matter what money troubles you have right now, you're still the best option for Marie. I think little angel helper wants you to be able to make the payment in time so that you can be done with those goons forever, and Marie can stay with you."

"That's conveniently what you want, too." He folded his arms.

Although that was true, it stung a little. Paulina wasn't trying to project her feelings onto Marie's guardian angel. She really believed that's why he kept stepping in. "Don't you want the same thing?"

"Of course. But I'm not unrealistic."

"I didn't tell Marie to have little angel helper find money for you."

"Exactly. I won't ask Marie to scavenge for forgotten bills. I'm sure there aren't anymore in there." With his thumb, he pointed back at his closet. "So that would probably mean taking cash from somebody else's pocket. Or . . . who knows?" He raised his arms, seeming frustrated. "I don't know how any of this works, and I don't think Marie should have to be bothered."

"Come by lil angel huppa." Marie gripped her own wrist, beckoning with the hand it was holding. "Let go."

This familiar phrase urged Paulina's hopes to continue

climbing. "When she's helping someone, that's what she says."

He held up his hands defensively. "This feels wrong. I don't want to use her like this."

"Use her?" For a moment, Paulina considered his statement. "Okay, I see what you mean. Marie is not some magic lamp that you rub when you've got problems. I think that's why little angel helper is willing to help you. Because you understand that. We've had parents come to TACA trying to get Marie to perform for them, and it never works. She's not an actress or a magician or a genie. But she does have an angel friend that I believe God sent to her, and I think he wants to take us somewhere. Why not just see? He's never led Marie to stealing. I don't think he'd start now."

Bradley glanced between Paulina and Marie, who still beckoned. "I don't know."

Why was he being so stubborn? "What can it hurt? She and I are going to be here until tomorrow evening. Think of it as spending more time with her before . . . you make any final decisions."

"I've made my decision. I don't see how it could possibly change, no matter where she takes us."

"Neither of us knew about the claw game either. Just keep an open mind. That's all I ask."

"Fine. Open mind. But please don't keep pushing if what happens doesn't change my mind. Sending her back is already breaking my heart. I don't want to be pushed anymore, okay?"

Paulina pressed her lips together. She *was* being pushy. "Sorry. I won't." But she was still hopeful, even if he wasn't.

"I think I'll change into these jeans after all. Give me a minute. Then we'll go."

13.

On the walk to the subway where Marie was apparently leading them, Bradley felt the knot that had formed in his stomach enlarging, pushing up into his diaphragm.

Marie skipped, clapped, pointed out the sights that awed her, and joyfully chattered along the way. Bradley picked up on a few words, but much of her phrasing was lost on him. It made him feel sick that he didn't have enough time to learn more of her language to the point where he understood it better. He'd thought of so many places to take her in the city where she'd enjoy the sights and sounds. All the restaurants he'd been sure would delight her, the shops, Central Park. Unlike most people, Marie was easy to please, quick to love, and bubbling over with cheerfulness.

The knowledge of her inevitable departure left a void inside him. His heart hurt. His head hurt. Everything wrong was his fault. He already dreaded having Marie leave and would miss her terribly. Never before had he minded living alone. He'd preferred it, in fact. Now he knew his place would feel empty without her.

Paulina strolled beside his sister, her dark ponytail bouncing against the back of her jacket collar. She responded to some of the things Marie said. She understood Marie a lot better than Bradley did. At least Marie would still have Paulina and her other friends at TACA.

Despite Paulina's obstinacy and passive aggression, he admired her more than any other woman he'd ever met besides his own mother. She had the most incredible patience with Marie, and him for that matter. Even in the midst of hopelessness, Paulina held onto her faith and hope that things could still work out.

Bradley couldn't allow himself to hope. It would be too painful to be disappointed yet again. Not that the disappointment would be Marie's fault, or her little angel helper's, or Paulina's. No, this was all on him and his poor choices.

At the Pelham Parkway subway entrance, Marie pointed. "Lil angel huppa. Dare."

"Any idea where this will take us?" Paulina turned back to Bradley.

He shrugged. The green line went toward downtown.

The possibilities were infinite.

Paulina insisted on paying for Marie. "Remember, I said I'd cover her expenses while I was here. No argument."

Bradley had pulled out his credit card at the machine. "Okay." Arguing with Paulina didn't seem like a good idea. She knew he couldn't really afford anything right now, no matter how cheap, so he appreciated her continued generosity. He already dreaded the arrival of his next credit card bill.

The pair of them went through the turnstiles, Marie giggling. Bradley swiped his MetroCard before pushing through the rotating bar. Marie led them to the platform where the next train would be arriving any time.

Although curious about their destination, Bradley still didn't think this little adventure would change his mind.

While riding the subway back to his apartment to break the bad news to Paulina and Marie, Bradley had come to the conclusion that he'd have to borrow the money from a friend, someone who wouldn't tack on interest. Paulina had been so sweet to offer, but he couldn't take her money. She'd already done so much for Marie, and he didn't want to cause her any more stress.

In the morning, he'd swing by his old office and speak to Drake about it. Bradley was tired of having no phone, but telling Drake in person seemed like the best way to ask to borrow $833. Drake had no idea about the gambling, but he'd never been a judgmental type. Bradley really hoped he'd be willing to help him out, and keep him accountable to never go back to that casino again.

After his encounter with Mario and Pauly, Bradley had been cured. Still it couldn't hurt to have someone to talk to in the future if any urges arose.

Even if Drake said yes, Bradley still couldn't allow Marie to stay. The problem? He didn't think Mario and Pauly would ever really let him off their hook. The threat was too blatant, implied though it was, for Bradley to feel safe from them ever again. He'd potentially be living the rest of his life looking over his shoulder, and that meant Marie would never be safe with him either. The thought of anyone hurting her . . .

Bradley stiffened, clenching his fists as they stood waiting for the train. No, he'd never put Marie in danger. As much as he hated to send her to the group home, at least she'd be safe there.

As the train approached, slowing to a stop in front of them, Marie waved at all the people sitting inside. A few waved back.

They rode as far as 149th Street – Grand Concourse before Marie said, "Off." Then she had them get on another train, the red line, which went into Manhattan. As they rode, passing station after station, Bradley had an inkling that they might be headed back to his office building, and shared the thought with Paulina.

"Really? Could you have left any money behind? Maybe you can pick up your last paycheck early!" Her eyes widened as she broadly grinned. She was pretty when she smiled. She had perfectly straight, white teeth behind her red lips. Her brown eyes were striking, too, which he hadn't really noticed until now as he sat shoulder to shoulder with her on the subway. Maybe it was the darkness of her tan skin that showcased the white teeth, the whites of her eyes, and the brown irises. "That's going to be enough, isn't it?"

"More than enough, but I already asked my boss that question when he fired me. They couldn't cut the check early, so I told him to send it direct deposit as usual."

Paulina scrunched up her brow, apparently thinking. "Maybe if you ask again you can change his mind?"

"I'd rather not." Bradley almost told Paulina about the possibility that Marie was taking him to the office so he could talk to Drake, but wanted to wait and see first. If that's where they were going, they still had quite a lot of time on the train. Bradley wanted to get something off his chest. "You know, I wasn't a good son to my parents. And they died not knowing how sorry I am that I pushed them away. I feel really guilty about that."

"You pushed them away?" Paulina turned her shoulders so that she faced him.

Marie was sitting quietly, staring out the windows with her mouth slightly open.

"In college, I did something really bad. I stole ten thousand dollars from them." He paused with his head down, staring at his Adidas shoes. He glanced up to check Paulina's reaction.

She raised one of her dark eyebrows. "Oh."

"Yeah. I think they probably knew, but I never confessed that it was me. Instead, I told them that I was tired of them always hassling me, and I didn't want a relationship with them anymore. I wanted to be on my own in New York, and asked them not to interfere with my life. They didn't understand, but they honored my request. Even if they knew about the money, I think what I said broke their hearts even more." Of course it had. Especially his mother's. "They would still call me every once in a while, but I wouldn't answer. That's why I didn't know about my mom's seizure. And why I haven't been in Marie's life for so long. I regret that as much as I regret what I did to my parents."

Paulina was quiet, gazing at him with compassion.

"All this time, I had chance after chance to tell them the truth. Now they're dead." He folded his hands in his lap, surprised how sharing relieved a burden that had always weighed on him. "Soon Marie will be gone. I'm getting what I deserve, really. I was the one who wanted to be left alone."

"I'm so sorry." Paulina's hand touched the back of his neck. She gave a gentle squeeze. It felt nice. "But you know something? I never heard an unkind word about you from either of them. I had no idea you weren't on speaking terms. Your mom especially was so proud. She talked about you a lot. How successful you were here in New York, all your hard work as an accountant, and that you'd soon be a CPA."

How did Mom know? She could've been assuming. Before the estrangement, he'd told her his plan was to get certified.

"They loved you. Marie always lit up when she talked about 'big bo Bad-lee.'"

The comfort Paulina gave him felt unearned. But he appreciated knowing these things. "Thanks, Paulina."

"You're welcome."

Suddenly, Marie stood up. "Off."

They were at the stop near the office where he'd been fired that morning. Now he was almost certain they were headed there. But why?

14.

Paulina rose to her feet when Marie stood and announced it was time to get off. They were at the 96th Street station. Bradley followed them as they exited the train. Out of the station, Paulina glanced over her shoulder to see if Marie was heading the direction he went for work. Rather, where he used to work.

"Yeah, this is the way. So far." He obviously didn't want to influence Marie, so he stayed behind as they walked ahead of him. The streets were busy compared to what Paulina was used to in Topeka. Lots of pedestrians. They had to weave a little bit to pass groups of people. At crosswalks, she was especially mindful of Marie, who had gone into "follow the angel" mode. At least that's how she and the Hunters used to refer to it. Marie's determined if uneven gait and her disinterest with her surroundings convinced Paulina that she could see the guardian she dubbed "lil angel huppa" leading her.

Paulina wondered what he did to make Marie follow him somewhere. Waved with his halo? Why would he lead them to Bradley's old office? Paulina hoped his last paycheck was the reason. His boss should have some compassion and give him a check. That would solve Bradley's problem. Maybe he'd change his mind again?

Bradley caught up to them on a wider sidewalk. Marie turned right, and Bradley intercepted. "I wanted to make sure she stopped. This is where I make my turn, too. Used to. I keep forgetting I don't work there now."

"Dis." Marie pointed down the street she had been about to cross. "Lil angel huppa dare."

Paulina's heart skipped, relieved that Bradley had the foresight to stop Marie from barging in front of traffic.

"I know, Marie. We have to wait until the sign changes," he said.

"She turned so suddenly." Paulina covered her forehead, not quite recovered from the possibility of what could've happened.

"I made sure I got between her and the street for that reason."

"So it has to be your office, right?"

"We're close now. But this is Marie's thing. She'll have to show us."

As they crossed the street, Paulina reflected on what Bradley had confided to her on the subway. He hadn't said why he took ten thousand dollars from his parents, and she didn't think she should ask. But whatever led him to it, he obviously felt remorse and regretted the action. Everything she told him was true. The Hunters gave no indication they were estranged from their son. They had obviously loved and missed him. Paulina hoped they were now at peace, and that they knew how their son really felt about them. That he loved them and missed them, too.

She felt led to confess something to him as well. "Bradley, you may not change your mind today. I understand that no matter what happens, I need to let that go. Also, there's something I want to tell you. I'm very sorry I cannot become Marie's guardian myself."

He turned to her as they walked. "What do you mean? I would never have expected you to."

He wouldn't? "Oh. Well, it's something I've thought about throughout the years for many of the TACA members. But my mother's an alcoholic and she lives with me. It's not a good environment for anyone else." Sometimes she included herself in that statement. But she couldn't abandon Mamá. "I don't have an extra room. It's a small apartment. My mom and I sleep in the same bedroom, and—"

"Paulina, you have nothing to apologize for." Bradley's face, with the softening of his eyes, indicated that he felt for her and wanted to reassure her. "I never would've asked anyone who wasn't family to take care of Marie. If you had been in a position to take care of her and offered yourself as an alternative to the group home, of course that would've been great. But it's not something I expect of you. It's me that I'm disappointed with. Never with you." He faced forward again, sighing. "I'll never feel safe because of these men, and I won't put Marie in harm's way. That's why I can't see anything changing my mind."

The way he tightened his mouth, his eyes narrowing with a mix of sadness and anger, Paulina knew he was hurting. She understood what he was saying, and could acknowledge that he might be wise in his decision. She wouldn't want Marie to be in harm's way either. But poor Bradley. To be scared all the time? That was no kind of life. She wished there was something she could do. Whatever little angel helper had in mind, she hoped he could somehow get Bradley out of this position.

Bradley glanced at the glass doors of a familiar building. "We're passing my office."

It was true. Marie kept walking. "So she wasn't leading you there after all. Any idea where she might be headed now?" Paulina asked.

"I have an idea. I'll keep it to myself because I still don't want to influence her. But if it's where I think, I'm not hopeful it will help us."

15.

As Marie continued to guide them past the office building, the smells of the pizza place next door filled the air, making Bradley's stomach growl. They should find a place to eat after . . . whatever was about to happen.

Bradley gave up his remaining hope for anything miraculous. He hadn't meant to allow himself to hope, but realized that something like desire crept inside his thoughts. A desire for a miracle. If she was going where he thought, the destination wasn't likely to yield anything miraculous.

A sing-songy tune resounded from Paulina's purse. Bradley glanced down at her, but she didn't make a move to answer her phone.

"It's probably Mamá. I can talk to her later."

They passed a storefront that sold purses at an average

cost of $50,000. That kind of money for a handbag. Bradley couldn't comprehend it. He caught Paulina gazing inside, but she quickly faced forward again. He wondered if she knew how expensive the purses lining the store window were, if that's why she didn't allow herself to stare.

Across one more street, and Marie lifted her arm, pointing at a sign about a hundred yards down the block. "Dare! Lil angel huppa. Dare! Dare!" She skipped toward the sign, her hand still pointing at it. She stopped near the entrance to Brevard Bank.

Like Bradley had thought.

"This bank?" Paulina patted Bradley's shoulder. "Do you know it?"

"It's my bank."

"Really?" Paulina waited, expecting something from him.

What? What could she and little angel helper possibly expect? "Yes. What now?"

Marie stared up at the sign, babbling. Bradley caught "lil angel huppa" but not much else. Then she noticed other things, like a carriage heading toward Central Park, only three blocks away. "Hosey!" She laughed and clapped, waving at the horse pulling the carriage. The driver waved back, tipping his top hat. A couple snuggled inside.

"Do you think Marie will be able to give us any other

clues?" asked Bradley.

"She's out of her 'follow the angel' mode, so I don't think so. This is where we're supposed to be. Maybe . . ." Paulina leaned, balancing on one foot. She peeked in through the glass door of the bank's entrance without moving in front of it. The rest of the building was brick overlay.

"What do I do? Take out a loan from them?" No, thanks. Bradley preferred to try a friend like Drake who wouldn't charge interest.

"No, I think," Paulina pointed at the ATM machine next to the glass door, "you should check your balance."

Waste of time. "Why? I know it. Like I told you, I only have a hundred bucks left to my name."

"Humor me." Paulina took his arm, leading him toward the machine. "Just check."

Her face was bright. She sounded light, as if it was no big thing for Bradley to keep reminding himself that he had almost no money. Not to mention that he owed some sketchy characters nearly a thousand dollars. Was she hoping this would be the miracle? Some kind of error at his bank would cause the balance inquiry to reflect a thousand or even ten thousand because somebody put the period in the wrong place?

"Look, Paulina, I know what it's going to say. I don't

really want to keep dredging it up."

"Please? Do it for Marie. She brought us here for a reason." Paulina's dark ponytail hung over her shoulder with the slightest curl at the end.

Marie walked up to Bradley, patting his arm. "Bad-lee. See? Lil angel huppa."

Marie's crooked smile and the way Paulina gently squeezed his hand softened him up, despite his hesitance. "Fine." He pulled out his ATM card. "I'll check. But then let's get out of here and find something to eat."

The sing-songy tune from Paulina's purse chimed in again. "Ugh, *Mamá*." She stepped back, raising one finger as she dug into her handbag. "Let me make sure she hasn't burned the place down."

"It's fine." Bradley inserted his card into the machine. He entered his pin number.

"Oh. It's not her." She came back to stand beside him and Marie. "I don't usually answer numbers I don't recognize. I'll let it go to voicemail."

As he pressed buttons on the screen, making a balance inquiry selection, Marie hung on his arm, swaying, nearly pulling him away from the machine. "Hang on, Marie. Let me just . . ." The account balance flashed on the screen.

$100.00.

No surprises there. Then why did Bradley feel

disappointed?

"Oh." Paulina sounded as deflated as he felt. "So that wasn't it. Maybe . . . I don't know."

"Listen, Paulina," said Bradley, trying to keep the mood light. "It's fine. Marie probably needed an adventure. Little angel helper wanted her to get out of the apartment, have a nice walk, and see some sights." He didn't add, "Since she won't get to do that again after tomorrow."

"But this isn't usually what happens. I guess there is no usual. But—"

Bradley placed his hands on each of their shoulders. "Hey, let's not spoil the time we have left. Let's find a nice place to eat dinner. There's this awesome Greek restaurant right around the corner. What do you say?"

Paulina sighed, nodding. "Sure. But let me take care of it, okay?"

"No, no. You've done enough of that. I want you to know that I've got a friend who can probably help me out with what I owe tomorrow. With my paycheck coming in, I'll be able to pay off my credit card bill when it comes no problem. Let me treat you two for once." He ushered them forward. "This way."

Paulina moved with him, but Marie slipped out of his grip.

"No, Bad-lee."

He turned back, both he and Paulina halting. "Come on, Marie. Let's go have some yummy Greek food."

"No!" she shouted.

"Hey, it's okay. We can do something else." Bradley approached cautiously, unsure what had upset her. "Do you like Italian better?"

"No!" She stomped her foot, pointing at the bank sign again. "Lil angel huppa."

"Is he . . . still there?" Bradley asked, gazing up but not seeing whatever held Marie's gaze.

Paulina wrapped her arm around Marie's shoulder, looking up at the sign. "Does little angel helper want us to stay here, Marie?"

"Yeah." She nodded, still pointing. "Dare."

Bradley and Paulina stared at each other, her seemingly at a loss like Bradley. "This isn't the usual lost and found situation, is it?" he asked.

"No," said Paulina. "When she finds the lost item, that's the end of it. She's never done anything like this before. But this isn't quite the same. I shouldn't have expected it to be, I guess."

"What do we do now?" Bradley's stomach growled. He really wanted a gyro and a Greek salad.

"I don't know." Paulina stretched out a weak smile. "Wait a little bit? A few minutes, at least."

"Okay. Sure. We can wait."

But for how long? And for what?

16.

Bradley leaned against the brick wall, gazing up and down the street. He took out his house keys, tossing them in the air, catching them. A few cabs passed. A bus or two. Some cars, people on bikes, a few pedestrians. Paulina and his sister stood in front of him on the sidewalk, Paulina attempting to draw some insight from Marie. He couldn't tell if she was getting anywhere or not.

His stomach rumbled. After five minutes of waiting for whatever little angel helper had in mind, he was ready to head to dinner at the Greek restaurant. The way Marie reacted before made him hesitate to push her. She'd gotten so upset when they walked away from the bank. But what were they waiting for? What did little angel helper's apparent perch on the bank sign even mean?

Bizarre and unlikely scenarios crossed his mind. Somebody on the roof would drop cash from the sky.

Somebody exiting the bank would feel an incredible urge to give them money. Somebody famous, like Al Pacino, would walk by. Marie would charm him, and he'd hand Bradley a blank check to make sure that sister of his was taken care of. Plus he knew some guys who could handle Bradley's loan sharks so they never bothered him or Marie again.

Bradley couldn't help but smile at that last one. He could admit that scenario would change his mind. With an upward glance, tossing his keys high, he silently sent a message to little angel helper.

Is that what we're waiting for? Because I really do want to be Marie's guardian. Make your move, will you?

"On the phone?" asked Paulina.

Marie was holding up her fist to her ear with her thumb sticking out. Her version of a phone, Bradley assumed.

"Little angel helper made the 9-1-1 call for your mom when she fell down. Does he need to make another phone call?"

Marie shook her head no, holding out her fist. "Lil angel huppa. Call."

Bradley straightened up as something struck his thoughts. He walked up to them. "Marie, does Paulina need to check her cell phone?"

She nodded, pushing her fist to her ear. "Call."

"What about that call you got earlier?" he asked. "It was

a number you didn't recognize. Did they leave a message?"

Paulina dug into her purse, lifting the cell phone out and staring at the screen. "Yes, they did."

Marie clapped, giggling as Paulina held the phone to her ear. "Yeah! Lil angel huppa. Call."

Bradley ruffled Marie's hair. "So Paulina's mystery caller is going to solve our problems, huh?" Sadly, he doubted it. Who would call Paulina that might be able to help?

Bradley kept up the key toss, biding time while she accessed her voicemail.

Paulina stared at the sidewalk, listening, and suddenly gasped. She covered her mouth, slowly lifting her chin, meeting Bradley's questioning gaze.

He didn't interrupt, waiting to ask what she was hearing. Her eyes didn't give away whether the surprise was happy or not.

She hung up the call without saying anything, and then started dialing someone.

With both hands raised, keys resting on top of his right palm, he waited for her to explain. "Who are you calling?" he asked. "What was it?"

She reached out, squeezing his left hand with a smile climbing up her cheeks.

"Good news?" he asked.

She nodded, not yet replying. "Hello!" she said into her phone, releasing his hand. "Can I please speak to Arthur Gorenstein?"

Bradley scrunched his brow. Who was that?

"Yes, hello, Mr. Gorenstein. My name is Paulina Robart. I received your message. I have Bradley Hunter right here."

What was going on? All Bradley could do was wait for her to fill him in.

"I'll let you speak to him directly." Paulina handed the cell phone over. "It's for you. He'll explain." She was suppressing her smile, but he could see it in her eyes.

He was at a total loss when he took the phone. With the cell at his ear, he said, "Hello? This is Bradley Hunter."

"Mr. Hunter. My name is Arthur Gorenstein." The voice reminded him of his granddaddy's, deep and crackly. "I'm the attorney handling the estate of David and Elaine Hunter, your late parents. Let me begin by saying I'm very sorry for your loss."

"Thank you." Bradley's mind raced, almost spinning off the rails. It never occurred to him that his parents would've left him anything. Not after the way he treated them. He tried to stop thinking about the possibilities, but couldn't help it. Had they left him something? They must have or Mr. Gorenstein wouldn't be calling.

"I apologize for the amount of time it has taken me to

track you down. I didn't have updated information on your home address, cell phone, or work number."

The last known address his parents would've had was in Queens, and he'd moved several times since then. He'd had the same cell number for a long time, but over three months ago had to close the account and get rid of the phone. The last his parents knew, he worked as an accountant at a non-profit, a home for battered women. Since then, he'd worked at two different firms, including his most recent job. No wonder it took the lawyer over two weeks to track Bradley down. But how did he get Paulina's number?

"It occurred to me that your sister, Marie, would likely be in your custody now, so I called her guardianship agency and received Paulina Robart's information. Again, I apologize that I couldn't reach you sooner."

Mr. Gorenstein apparently read his thoughts. But he wasn't to blame for Bradley's estrangement with his parents. "No apology needed." He waited, not sure what questions to ask, hoping the attorney would continue explaining his reason for the call.

"Then I'll get straight to the point, Mr. Hunter. Your parents left you a small sum of money."

Small sum. What did a lawyer consider small? Bradley didn't want to, but he couldn't help but ask, "How much?"

"Well, now that the estate sale at the home is over, I can

give you an exact amount. They didn't have many assets, and the money they had in the bank mostly went toward funeral costs. In their living will, they wanted any money left to go to you. The amount is—"

Dun. Dun.

"Wait, what?" asked Bradley.

"I said—"

Dun. Dun.

Bradley pulled the phone away from his ear. What was wrong with the sound?

Someone was calling in, and the tone was interrupting. The caller ID read, *Mamá.*

"Oh." Bradley glanced at Paulina, showing her the screen. "Your mom is beeping in. Do you need to talk to her?"

"No! I'll call her later." Paulina waved the backs of her hands at him. "Finish talking."

Bradley squeezed the keys in his hands, more anxious now, and put the phone to his ear again. The other call apparently went to voicemail.

"Hello? Mr. Hunter, are you there?"

"Yes, I'm sorry. There was another call. Do you mind repeating the amount?"

"Of course. The amount is eight hundred and thirteen dollars."

Bradley dropped the keys. They clanked on the sidewalk. His mouth fell open. "I'm sorry. Did you say, 'eight hundred and thirteen dollars'?"

Paulina was holding Marie's hand, but at Bradley's statement, she covered her mouth.

"That's right. The amount can be wired to whatever account you'd like, but first I need to fax you the paperwork to sign. Do you have access to a fax machine?"

Bradley slowly twisted, lifting his chin and staring at the Brevard Bank sign. He could imagine a little cherub perched on top of it, smiling down at him. "I don't, but I'm at the bank."

"Perfect! If you can find out their fax number, we can get this settled right away."

"Okay. I'll call you back." As Bradley lowered the phone from his ear, he shoved one hand into his jeans pocket. Slowly, he lifted out the twenty dollar bill. It was the bill Marie had led him to in his closet, the forgotten twenty bucks that she found for him.

Twenty plus eight hundred and thirteen equaled . . .

"Eight-three-three," he said aloud. Exactly the amount he owed to Mario and Pauly.

Again, he stared at the bank sign, searching for little angel helper. The coincidences were too many for him to explain away. The belief that a guardian angel was really there, watching over Marie, settled on him like a wave of peace. He couldn't take his eyes off the sign.

He almost thought he could see something. Almost.

17.

The clanking of Bradley's keys on the sidewalk startled Paulina. As Bradley lowered the phone from his ear, he turned away from her to stare at the bank sign. Paulina restrained her enthusiasm, waiting.

$813. Was that the amount his parents had left him?

When Paulina heard Mr. Gorenstein's voice message, she'd been so hopeful that this was the reason little angel helper had led them to the bank. Could Bradley withdraw the amount right away? Would he change his mind?

All the questions bubbled up inside Paulina, making her whole body tremble as she tried to hold them in. She held Marie's hand, squeezing every few seconds to make sure she didn't let go. The sweet girl swayed, humming to herself, seeming much calmer than before.

Paulina couldn't stand the silence any longer. "Bradley!" she cried. "What did he say?"

He jumped, turning back to her, his face, an expression of bewilderment. "My parents left me money. Eight hundred and thirteen dollars." He held up his hand. The twenty dollar bill from his closet was crumpled in his fist. "I now have exactly eight-three-three. The amount I owe." Slowly, he lowered his fist, his eyes glazed over as if not quite believing the truth.

She knew it. "Sweet God in heaven," she breathed. "Another miracle." Little angel helper gave Bradley another reason to trust that everything would work out.

Bradley's eyes searched their surroundings as if seeking verification of Paulina's statement.

"Do you need any further proof, Bradley? Little angel helper led Marie here for this reason. Will you be able to withdraw the money now?"

"I'm not sure. Maybe once I receive and sign the paperwork."

"Does this . . ." Paulina hesitated. She'd promised not to push him anymore. "What does this mean?" A better way to approach him.

"It means I don't have to borrow the money, which does feel pretty miraculous right now." He bowed his head, staring at the twenty in his hand. "I can't believe they left me anything."

After his earlier confession, Paulina understood what

particularly had come to mind. The money he stole from his parents. "They loved you so much, Bradley. Nothing you did or didn't do could change that. Maybe this was their way of letting you know."

He raised his chin, sheepishly grinning. "Feels undeserved, you know?"

"I know why you think that, but no. Not undeserved at all." She stepped forward with Marie, touching his arm. "Shall we go inside?"

The bank was closing in forty-five minutes, but it was enough time for Bradley to sign the fax that Mr. Gorenstein sent and return it. The money would become available first thing in the morning. As far as Paulina's understanding, he could still pay the men he owed in time.

At dinner, Paulina poured Greek dressing on her and Marie's salad, large enough for them to share. Bradley hadn't said much as they left the bank and walked the short distance to the quaint restaurant. Inside, the walls were decorated with paintings of the Greek Isles. Outside where they were seated on the patio, the large trellis overhead was covered in vines and flowers.

Marie stabbed at a black olive, but her fork scraped the plate as the olive rolled away. "Aw, miss."

"Here, Marie." Bradley offered her the olive at the end of his own fork.

She took it off with her fingers and popped it into her mouth. "Mmm."

The pressure was building inside Paulina, making it difficult for her to hold in her thoughts. What was the best way to open the dialogue? He hadn't said anything about changing his mind, but Paulina wanted to find out for sure. And if not, why?

Maybe he wanted to eat first. Paulina had gotten pretty hungry as well, so she waited. About halfway through her portion of the salad, Bradley said, "This is good, isn't it?"

Paulina finished chewing and swallowed. "Yes. Excellent." She smiled, hoping this meant he was ready to talk. He'd almost finished his salad, but still had a gyro on his plate.

"I wanted Marie to have more time in the city. There are so many great restaurants. She would've loved Central Park." He picked up the gyro, opened the foil on one end, and then took a bite.

Paulina's heart crashed down into her stomach. That didn't sound like a change in Bradley's decision. He still intended to send Marie to the group home? She couldn't help but confess her disappointment. "You're really not going to be her guardian? Even after everything that's happened?"

The look on Bradley's face told Paulina he had dreaded

her reproach. "I believe now, Paulina. I really do. Little angel helper is real. He's watching over Marie, and he's going to make sure she's well provided for."

That was a surprise.

"Lil angel huppa," said Marie. She lifted a forkful of potato salad into her mouth, some of it left behind on the corners of her lips as she chewed with her mouth open.

Paulina thought he didn't believe, and that's why he wouldn't change his mind. "Everything he's done so far has been to make sure *you* are the one who can provide for her. The egg. The money in your closet. The inheritance. Isn't that enough to change your mind?" She spoke as gently as she could, holding back the side of her that wanted to shake him.

"I know what it must look like from your perspective." He reached out, placing his hand on top of hers. Her palm was down, fingers touching the table. The move served to comfort her, as must've been his intention. "And I'm so incredibly grateful for all that has happened today. Three miracles is way more than I deserve. But I also don't trust the men that I'll be paying tomorrow. I don't know if they'll come up with some other mystery amount that I owe them. They seem capable of anything. That's why I can't allow Marie to stay. I'll never trust them. I was an idiot for going to them in the first place. I'm more sorry than I can express that it means I can't be her guardian."

As he pulled his hand away, Paulina felt the cool air replace his warm palm. He was right in his desire to protect Marie. But didn't he think that if little angel helper went to all this trouble that he'd keep Marie safe? Paulina couldn't argue that point because Bradley was determined, not to mention practical.

There was nothing Paulina could say that would change Bradley's mind. She and Marie would be leaving tomorrow evening. He was as devastated about that fact as Paulina. She could tell by the remorse in his eyes. If he could go back and change things, he would. But he couldn't. There was no solution except to get Marie away from there. And it broke Paulina's heart.

18.

Bradley sat next to Marie on the subway ride back to his apartment. He tickled her, teased her, made her laugh as much as he could. At one point, she leaned over and wrapped him up in a bear hug. "Love you, Bad-lee."

"I love you, Marie."

Nothing could remove the wrench that had lodged in his heart. It was painful for him knowing that if he hadn't been so foolish, he could've been Marie's guardian.

Paulina smiled sadly as she watched them, not saying much. He couldn't blame her. She didn't want Marie in that group home any more than Bradley did. But little angel helper's miraculous provisions—he hated to say it—weren't enough. He didn't want Mario or Pauly even finding out he had a sister, let alone one that was visiting him in the city.

Back at the apartment, Paulina helped Marie change into

her pajamas. In bed, Marie snuggled up with her favorite stuffed bunny. Paulina knelt beside her and said a prayer. "Dear God, thank you for Marie, and thank you for her little angel helper."

"Huppa," said Marie.

"Give her good dreams. Amen."

"Pink bed. Men." Marie rolled onto her side, squeezing the bunny in her arms. "Nite, Bad-lee. Nite, Lee-na."

"Goodnight."

At the door, Bradley shut off the light. "Goodnight, Marie."

In the kitchen, he sipped a glass of water, thinking about his plan for the morning. He'd swing by his bank first and withdraw the money from the ATM. Then he'd head to Brooklyn, likely arriving at Pauly's around ten thirty.

Paulina quietly shut Marie's door. Bradley would probably think of his spare room as Marie's room from now on. "I'll call the airline in the morning and get Marie on my flight," she said.

"I'll pay with my credit card." That was the least he could do.

"You'll get reimbursed." Paulina opened the cupboard and took down a glass, filling it with water from the faucet.

They sat on the couch together.

"I'm sorry, Bradley." She set her glass down on the

coffee table. "I've been so pushy. I didn't understand that you wanted this for Marie as much as I did."

"You have nothing to apologize for. I'm sorry for failing to keep my word." He tilted his head back, draining the rest of the glass. He set it next to Paulina's. "You're an amazing person. All you do for people with special needs. All you've done for Marie. I can never thank you enough." He glanced at her, grinning.

She smiled her pretty smile, her eyes squinting. "I appreciate that, Bradley. To me, it's the best job in the world. But you have nothing to apologize for either. You love Marie. You're a good brother to her."

He didn't feel that way now, but he wouldn't argue. It was after ten, and he felt exhausted. "I think I'll head to bed." He automatically leaned forward to kiss her on the cheek.

She turned her face the direction he was moving. He kissed her lips. Her eyes widened and she leaned away, startled.

On the couch, he jumped back, putting space between them. "Sorry, I meant to kiss your cheek."

"Oh, it's fine. I'm Latina." She waved her hands in front of her face, making him think her statement was an attempt to cover her embarrassment, and his.

He cleared his throat. "Goodnight then."

Without raising her gaze from the glasses on the coffee table, she said, "Goodnight. I hope everything works out for you."

"Thanks, Paulina." As he walked away, his cheeks felt warm. He could still feel the impression of her lips on his. He'd probably never see her again. At least not for some time, which made him sad. She was really growing on him.

At ten thirty-five the next morning, Bradley approached Pauly's Laundry Service. In a grocery bag, the envelope from the bank contained $833. He pushed the door open and a bell chimed.

The dark-haired young man looked up from a newspaper on the counter. "Morning."

"Good morning. Is Mario here?"

"One sec." He picked up the phone on the counter and dialed a few numbers. "That guy is here. The one from yesterday. Right."

Bradley swallowed. The kid remembered him. What did he know? What was Mario saying?

He hung up the phone. "He'll be here in ten minutes. He wants you to wait."

"Sure." Bradley would do whatever Mario asked, waiting however long it took. He didn't think it'd be wise to leave even if he wanted to. Mario wasn't someone to refuse.

There was a chair beside the door. He sat with the grocery bag in his lap rolled tightly over the envelope. He tapped his foot. Fifteen minutes passed, then twenty. He was getting more and more anxious.

"Hey." The kid jerked his thumb into the air. "Go on back."

Bradley rose to his feet and strode past the hanging laundry. The door in the back was open.

Mario's hand beckoned from inside. "Hunter, I didn't expect you this soon. Shut the door, will ya?"

Bradley didn't want to, but he did, immediately turning back to Mario. He wore a suit today. It looked like Armani. Bradley had never seen Mario in a suit.

"Ah. I know. Funeral. I hate these things." He waved over the outfit. "Makes me feel like some kind of Wall Street bug. Somebody with hive mentality waiting to be squashed. That's not me. I'd rather make a statement that says don't mess with me. You know?"

Bradley nodded. He knew. "It's all here." He held out the money.

Mario took the grocery bag without looking inside. "You got eight eighty-three that fast? I'm impressed."

Even with a ceiling fan blowing air over him, Bradley was sweating. "Eight *thirty*-three. I gave you fifty dollars yesterday, on top of the rest."

"Did you?" Mario tossed the bag onto his desk. "I don't remember that."

This was no less than Bradley anticipated, but the smug look on Mario's face was infuriating. He didn't want to play these games anymore.

"Tell you what," Mario stroked his chin, "get the fifty you owe me in the next three hours, and I'll forget that you came to me short."

No. *No!*

Mario pretending he didn't take that extra fifty yesterday was right on par with what Bradley expected, but it still enraged him. He controlled the anger as best he could, taking slow, deep breaths. "My debt is paid in full, including thirty percent interest. I handed you that extra fifty yesterday, and I know you remember taking it."

"You know I remember? You got balls, Hunter, I'll give you that. So let me give you a piece of advice. Look at that fifty you still owe as the reminder you obviously need that you're *never* paid in full." He patted Bradley's shoulder, hard. "Lucky for you, I'm in a generous mood. Funeral, life, death, and all that. So get that fifty to me whenever you can. Better yet, take out another K and get over to the casino. The way you're collecting cash lately makes me think you're on some kind of a lucky streak. I'm willing to bet on you."

Bradley was trapped. Mario would never let him go. He would bully Bradley until he got indebted to him again. Bradley steeled himself, straightening his posture and setting his jaw. "I'm clear and free. Everything I owe you is in that envelope. I'm walking out of here, and I'm never coming back." Now seemed like the moment to make good on that promise and walk away. But Bradley's shoes felt glued to the floor.

Mario raised his caterpillar eyebrows. Then he burst out laughing. "Oh, man. I never saw you as the type to take a stand. Forgive me for laughing, but your face . . ." He chuckled again. "So serious." He sighed out the rest of his laughter. "Let me respond in kind."

He gripped Bradley's shoulder and squeezed. It didn't really hurt, but had the effect Mario intended. Bradley felt afraid. His beady eyes bore into Bradley's, sending his point home.

"You're a customer here, and you always will be. Your time at the casino is not without cost. I expect my share, or you should expect to receive a visit from Pauly and his brother. Trust me, you don't want that. Whether you're at the casino, or at your little fifth floor apartment in the

Bronx, or your Manhattan office at the Linex Firm, they will find you."

The peppermint Altoids scent on Mario's breath hit Bradley's hot face like a cold breeze. Mario knew where he lived. The former workplace and casino weren't concerns. But his apartment . . .

Bradley's only relief was that he'd been cautious about Marie. She'd be out of harm's way tonight. "I'm done with the casino. And I'm done with you." He shrugged off Mario's grip and turned to open the door.

"I see. Trying to quit. Normally, I would say good for you, but in this case, quitting is not good for you."

Bradley opened the door and marched out.

"I give you a week, Bradley. You'll be back at that casino. And sooner or later that will bring you back here. Trust me!"

Bradley walked briskly, avoiding eye contact with the kid up front.

"Hey, wait."

He would not wait. He was out of there, never coming back. If Pauly had a brother, those two were probably a frightening sight side by side. Bradley needed to talk to someone. Tell Drake what was going on. Then get a body guard. If only he could afford one.

"Your jacket, man. It's ready."

Bradley paused halfway out the door. He glanced back.

The kid held up his gray suit jacket. He completely forgot about dropping it off. That was fast. They didn't usually have his stuff ready in one day. He wasn't returning, so they would've ended up keeping his jacket, too. How convenient.

Too convenient. Bradley approached the counter. "I don't have my slip."

"It's cool, dude. I know it's yours. This is on the house. From Mario."

Bradley didn't like the sound of that. "I'll pay for it." He pulled out his credit card. "How much?"

"I can't charge you. Not when Mario tells me not to."

Bradley took the coat by the hanger. He removed the wrapping. He didn't know what exactly told him to do it, but he checked the pockets. In an outside pocket, he found the menu from the casino that Marie had colored. They must've put it back in after the cleaning. In the inside pocket, he found an envelope. Thick, stuffed with cash. "What's this?" He slapped the envelope down onto the counter.

"One K. For the casino."

$1,000? The kid was regurgitating Mario's words. He didn't know Bradley wasn't in the mood. Or if he knew, his face didn't give it away. This had been prepared beforehand. Mario must've known what Bradley was going to do. And he thought he'd snag him this way, if not face to face.

"No, I'm sorry. This isn't mine. I don't know what you're talking about." He left the envelope on the counter, tossing the wire hanger on top of it. He exited the building with his jacket.

"Get down on the ground!"

A group of men in blue coats rushed him. One grabbed him and pushed him down. His knees hit the sidewalk, his left one scraping and stinging. Some of the men barged past him and went inside.

"FBI! ON THE GROUND! HANDS BEHIND YOUR HEAD!"

Bradley obeyed, lowering onto his stomach and moving his hands behind his head. He couldn't think, he could only respond to the commands. His heart pounded into the concrete. He felt a knee in his back. Metal cuffs locked around his wrists. He was being pulled up. He knelt before standing to his feet, the left knee burning.

What was happening? The FBI was arresting him?

Stupid. Stupid. Stupid.

"This way," the agent said. He had wiry white hair. As he pushed Bradley into the back of a black van, he came in beside him, shutting the door. Bradley knelt, lowering to a half-seated position to ease his throbbing knee, his gaze darting around. There was no place to sit except the floor. The van had no seats besides the driver and passenger chairs, both occupied with two more agents in blue coats.

The cuffs were uncomfortable. He wanted them off. What were they arresting him for?

"Is this your wallet?" The white-haired agent raised a brown leather wallet that looked like Bradley's.

"I think so." Had it fallen out or had the guy taken it from his pocket?

He pulled out the license. "Bradley D. Hunter?"

"Yes."

"What business did you have today in Pauly's Laundry Service?"

"My coat." Not quite the honest truth, but the only thing he could think to say.

"This coat?" The woman in the driver's seat held up his gray suit jacket. He must've dropped it on the sidewalk in the confusion.

"Yes."

"You checked the pockets?" the white-haired guy asked.

"Only this." She unfolded Marie's coloring. "He's clean."

Thank God Bradley hadn't taken the money. What would they have done then? What would they do now?

"Is that the only reason you came to Pauly's today?"

Bradley took a moment to answer, which probably wasn't a good idea. He didn't think lying to an FBI agent was a good idea either. "I made the mistake of borrowing money from them."

"Who?"

"Mario and Pauly."

"How much?"

"Today I came in with eight hundred and thirty-three dollars, and that was the last of the money I owed them. But Mario threatened me. He knows where I live. I quit gambling. I'm trying to make a change here." Would they sympathize with him? Or would they see him as the scum of the Earth for associating with such men?

The white-haired agent glanced over Bradley's head. He twisted to look. The woman in the passenger seat pressed a cell phone to her ear, listening. "Good. Thanks, Travis." She lowered the phone. "The kid who works the front counter's talking. Spilling like a waterfall. We can cut this one loose."

Meaning . . . he was free to go?

The white-haired agent nodded. "Turn around."

Bradley did, scooting on his butt. The agent unlocked the handcuffs.

"Here's your coat." The woman reached between her

seat and the driver's, holding the jacket over the console.

Bradley took it. "Thanks." Out of the van, the agent returned Bradley's wallet. "So I'm not under arrest?"

Please let me go. Please.

"No."

"I'm not in trouble?" He had to be sure.

"We're here for the big catch, and your offenses can be overlooked this time."

"What happens now?"

"Take this golden ticket to the chocolate factory, and make those changes you were talking about. Looks like you've got someone else to think about, too." He gestured to the pocket that contained Marie's coloring. "Otherwise, you might not get so lucky next time."

Although the agent didn't have a golden ticket, or anything else in his hands, Bradley knew what he meant. "What about Mario and Pauly?"

"They're going to federal prison. For a long time," he added.

"Pauly's brother, too?"

"The brother, the uncle, the four idiot cousins, probably even the cat."

Bradley had never seen a cat inside.

"You don't have to worry about these guys anymore. You can live your life without fear." Something on the agent's neck glinted in the sunlight. A silver chain. Bradley followed it and saw a silver cross peeking out from the agent's collar.

"Do you believe in angels?" Bradley asked.

The agent furrowed his dark eyebrows, a contrast to his white hair. "I don't know. I believe in God, and angels come with the territory. So yeah, I guess so. Why?"

Bradley smiled, his heartbeat finally slowing from the adrenaline rush. "No reason."

19.

The first sensation Paulina felt was disbelief. Then shock. Those two came and left very quickly, replaced with indescribable joy. "Oh, my God!" She grabbed Bradley, squeezing him tight. "I can't believe it. You're really keeping Marie?"

"Yes. I'm her guardian now, and I'm not signing her over to the state. Not ever."

She hugged him again, tears filling her eyes and spilling down his shoulder. "I knew it had to have been for a reason. All the things little angel helper did. It wasn't for nothing."

"I'm safe, and Marie is safe. We've got an angel watching over us." He held her back from him, touching her damp cheek. "I'll never doubt that again."

She kissed his, remembering how embarrassed she'd felt the night before. None of that mattered now. Everything was working out better than she could ever have imagined.

At the airport, she held Marie as long as the sweet girl would let her. "I'll miss you very much, Marie."

The crooked smile faded, and Marie seemed to grasp some of what was happening. "Miss you, Lee-na."

"But I promise to come visit sometime soon. Okay?"

"Yeah!" She clapped, bouncing on her toes.

Paulina would hold onto that image, and remember it whenever she needed to make herself smile.

Bradley stood behind his sister, smiling shyly at the floor. "I hope you will come visit soon. We'd both really like to show you some more of the sights."

Maybe she could visit them during Christmas vacation. "I'll be in touch. Somehow." She giggled, not meaning to laugh at his lack of a phone. "You have email, right?"

"Yeah." He pulled out a business card. "Do you have a pen? My work email is on here, which I won't have access to anymore, but I have Yahoo as well." She handed him the pen from her purse, and he wrote his email address. "Write to me?"

He seemed to mean it, and Paulina felt flattered by his insistence. "I will. I promise." They hugged. He felt so warm and comfortable. When they parted, she waved to both Bradley and his sister. "Goodbye."

"Byebye!" Marie waved back.

"Oh, I forgot to tell you," she said to Bradley, "I circled

some CPA jobs in the newspaper. I left it out on your counter. One of them paid really well. The Packer Group, I think?"

"They're hiring? That's a place I've wanted to work since I got my degree." His smile lit up his entire face. His only other moments at that level of happiness involved Marie. "Wow, thanks, Paulina, for doing that. Come back soon, okay? There's always room for you at our place."

Paulina walked away smiling. It felt good to hear Bradley say "our place" in reference to the home he now shared with Marie. They were both going to be fine. Better than fine. And little angel helper would be there watching over them.

My sister, Aunie, who was the inspiration for Marie's character, and me during a visit with our oldest sister, Larisa, in Georgia.

Author's Note

Little Angel Helper originally appeared as a daily live story on my blog, Writing for the Love. I'd wanted to write a story with a character who has special needs, and a vague idea had formed. I'm a fan of a podcast called *The Dunesteef Audio Fiction Magazine*, and they had a writing prompt with the following statement: "Despite being warned about them, someone plays a claw vending machine game . . . and wins big." The idea I'd been mulling over meshed well with this writing prompt and led me to write *Little Angel Helper* one day at a time for seventeen days on my blog. Read more about my writing process in a post entitled, "Afterward: Inspiration for Little Angel Helper" at this web address:

http://briaburton.blogspot.com/2014/08/afterward-inspiration-for-little-angel.html